WHEN THE LADY MUST WED

JESSIE CLEVER

SOMEDAY LADY
PUBLISHING, LLC.

For Sarah

The Hodge Family Tree

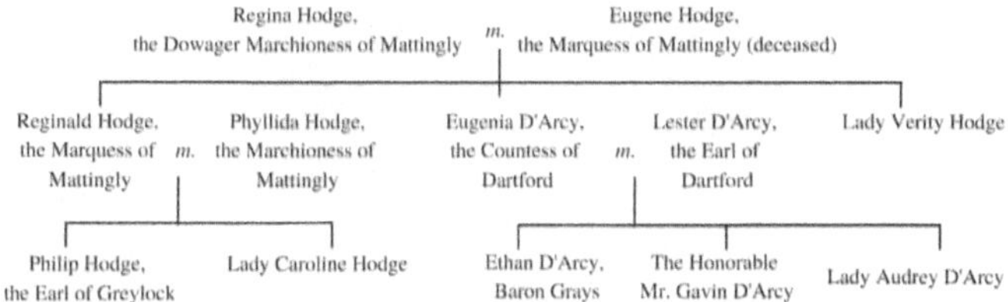

CHAPTER 1

*L*ady Winnaretta Lowe felt sick to her stomach when people praised her, as they often did, for helping her sister appear at her best in society.

Because she wasn't helping her sister out of the goodness of her heart. Not at all.

Lady Winnaretta Lowe was paying for her sins.

Sins that would have sent any proper society matron to her knees. Sins that had tarnished her family's reputation so badly it was all Winnie could do to prop it back up again.

Sins that required a penance so great she was giving her life for it.

In the form of marriage.

To the vilest man in society.

"Is Chichester coming today?" her mother said as if listening to the litany of Winnie's disparaging thoughts.

"Yes, Mother," she said, her eyes never straying from the spectacle on the Thames below. "I believe he had some gentlemen he wished to see here."

When Miles Creedmoor, the Marquess of Chichester, had first suggested they attend today's presentation, he had not mentioned a desire to see her. He had only mentioned a group of gentlemen he had been considering as potential investors for one of his real estate endeavors. It was no surprise that she hadn't seen him yet.

Her mother lazily fanned herself and pressed the backs of her fingers of her free hand to her forehead. It wasn't overly warm as it was only the middle of June, but the viewing platform on which they stood was crowded, verging on uncomfortable.

"Oh, that's lovely," her mother said without feeling. "He was so kind to secure us our places here." The older woman slid her a weighty look as it was no secret what Winnie was doing. Well, not the intent of it anyway. Her own reasons for doing it were very much a secret.

No, her family understood her pursuit of the Marquess of Chichester even if her father disagreed with it entirely, and her mother condoned it only so far as it aided the other Lowe daughter in securing a match. The same Lowe daughter who gave a soft snort to her left.

Winnie finally looked away from the parade of boats below them to find her sister hiding a derisive expression behind her own fan.

"Is it really so awful he's not here yet?" she murmured. Judging by the stricken look that came over her little sister's features when she found Winnie gazing at her, Ingrid had probably thought the comment would be lost in the cacophony of celebration.

Winnie frowned firmly enough to correct her sister, even though Winnie agreed with her comment. It was rather a relief that Chichester was not there yet. Perhaps for a little while longer Winnie wouldn't be reminded of her impending life sentence as Lady Winnaretta Creedmoor, the Marchioness of Chichester.

"Why is it that they're calling it the Strand Bridge? I thought we were commemorating our victory at Waterloo."

Winnie turned back to her mother. "You know how it is, Mother. The government does what it can to bolster morale."

Her mother turned then, and Winnie caught the line of perspiration burrowed in the rivets of face powder still visible across her forehead. Her mother still wore the stuff, in effusive layers no less, even when it had become less fashionable. "Bolster morale? We won, didn't we?"

Her mother meant no harm, but Winnie couldn't stop the sharp stab of memory that pierced her.

"Mother," Ingrid said sharply, leaning forward to peer around Winnie to give their mother a scathing glare.

"What?" her mother asked innocently enough, and Ingrid did little more than move her eyes in Winnie's direction.

Winnie shifted from foot to foot, curling her toes in her slippers as the wooden boards beneath her feet grew tiresome, hoping the movement would distract her from the exchange taking place in front of her.

Her mother made a dismissive snort. "It's been five years since he died. She can't possibly—"

"William." The name sprang from her lips no matter how she tried to blank her mind against it, to steel herself from the torment it brought with it, but it couldn't be stopped. The turmoil that brewed inside of her, the turmoil stoked by her sins, would not let William's death go unmarked even when it cost her to speak his name.

Because when she spoke the name of her dead lover, her heart beat with the name of someone else.

Philip.

She closed her eyes against the pain, still so fresh even now five years later. A sudden breeze swept through the viewing platform, and she forced her eyes open, the air reviving if not refreshing as it lay heavy with the scents of sea and fish, salt and brine. It worked though, and soon she had a better grip on her emotions, enough so to look her mother in the eye.

"His name was William, Mother. And I will always love him."

Liar.

She bit the inside of her cheek and looked resolutely out at the water where a parade of Navy vessels was just approaching the newly built Strand Bridge.

Her mother's hand settled on her arm, bringing her attention back to the woman. She found her mother's face folded in concern, but there was something else in her eyes, something that almost looked like regret.

"I know, dear. I know," she said.

Further conversation was forestalled with the sudden clang of cymbals from the band playing somewhere below them. It was really a spectacle. All of this pomp and circumstance for a bridge the government couldn't afford. Her father had told her as much. She looked about their little group, wishing he were there, but he had sought out a position closer to the actual bridge, hoping to study its engineering at a closer distance. It was left to her to watch her little sister and their mother. Although, with a glance in Ingrid's direction, Winnie felt her heart squeeze.

Her sister was little no longer. Wasn't that how Winnie had come to find the punishment that fit her crime?

"Where are Lord and Lady Snowshill? I thought they would be here today," she said then, effectively changing the subject. She knew they were to be there. Chichester had gotten them admission to the viewing platform as well.

Ingrid smiled genuinely for the first time since they'd squeezed their way onto the platform. "Robert sent me a note this morning that they would be somewhat delayed. His mother had torn a shoe and was having it mended."

"Torn a shoe? Doing what?" their mother said over the smashing of cymbals from the band that could be heard but not seen.

The abrupt change in volume shook the viewing platform, the boards beneath Winnie's feet vibrating ominously, and she suddenly wished her father were there. Her eyes drifted to the beams overhead, to the posts marking the four corners of the packed space. Her father would know if the thing were properly built.

As it was, Ingrid put out a hand as if to grab hold of something for support when another hand reached through the throng and grabbed it. For a moment Winnie stood mesmerized by that single hand reaching out from the crowd, seeming to sense her sister's need without hesitation. Her heart thudded in her chest, her stomach tightening at the sight.

Only someone in love could sense another's needs like that. She knew because once someone had reached for her hand without her realizing she needed it.

Philip.

The name reverberated through her like a painful echo, but Philip wasn't there today. Philip wasn't there anymore at all. She'd made sure of that.

Robert Clarke, the son of Viscount Snowshill, stepped from the crowd as if summoned.

Winnie couldn't stop a smile in greeting. Robert was tall and broad of shoulder, which may have been intimidating if not for his soft features, his warm brown eyes, and his lazy smile. There was something so good and pure about Robert Clarke, and Winnie couldn't wait for him to marry Ingrid.

Her smile vanished though as Lord and Lady Snowshill followed their son through the crowd, stepping into the small space in front of Winnie and blocking what little view she'd had.

She greeted the two politely enough even as her stomach tightened in instinctual protection for her sister.

Winnie met Lady Snowshill's eye as she smiled without warmth. "I trust you are well, Lady Snowshill."

The problem was Lord and Lady Snowshill had not given Robert their blessing to propose to Ingrid, citing concern for Ingrid's family. Winnie knew what their true meaning was in such a cloaked statement. They were concerned about Winnie and her reputation. But Winnie had found the answer to assuaging their concern, and he stepped through the crowd at that very moment.

Miles Creedmoor, the Marquess of Chichester, towered above the crowd. Tall and sinewy, he never failed to remind Winnie of a dried-out piece of leather. This was probably reinforced by the fact that he was twenty years her senior.

Winnie swallowed as she prepared herself to accept Chichester's greeting.

"Lady Bibury," he said with a bow to her mother first and then Lord and Lady Snowshill. Finally he turned to the younger set, Winnie, Ingrid, and Robert, and when his gaze landed on her, she felt her stomach clench.

"Lady Winnaretta," he intoned, and she couldn't stop the feeling that he had seen something desirable in a window shop and planned to procure it at any cost.

She would have been revolted by the covetous look in his eye except when Lord and Lady Snowshill had proclaimed their concern for the Lowe family, they had also presented a solution. When they had denied their blessing, they had informed Robert that the Lowes were not of the same ilk as some others in society, namely the Marquess of Chichester, whom they revered for his innovation and intellect.

It had only been a matter of social positioning to place Winnie directly in the marquess's sights when the season began so many weeks ago. She let him take her hand now as he placed a kiss on her kid glove. So many weeks and already a proposal was imminent. She just had to stay the course a little longer.

But then he dropped her hand, his gaze already moving behind her.

"Wallston!" Chichester called before he pushed Winnie out of the way to move through the crowd at her back.

She blinked, noting the stricken look on her mother's and Ingrid's faces, but Winnie forced a smile and turned to Lady Snowshill.

"I trust you are enjoying today's celebrations."

Lady Snowshill did little more than wave a hand in recognition, her attention already taking in the other women on the platform rather than the parade of boats on the Thames below them. "Fine, fine. Where is Lady Huxley? She promised to be in attendance."

"Winnifred!" Lord Snowshill blustered through the broom of his mustache.

Winnie only smiled. She'd corrected Robert's father a number of times and had rather given up on doing so anymore. He could go on thinking her name was Winnifred for all it mattered.

"I say, what a show," Lord Snowshill went on, jostling to turn about and face the river. "What a show, I say." He'd almost made it completely about when his elbow struck Winnie directly in the ribs, sending her backward.

She pressed a hand to where the offending joint had connected, pain smarting along her side, but she caught sight of Robert and Ingrid, pressed scandalously close together, her sister's face upturned to his, and there—there Winnie saw something she had once known herself.

Love.

Pure, uncomplicated love.

Winnie couldn't stop the smile that turned up the corners

of her lips at seeing her sister so happy. But the smile didn't linger as Winnie turned her attention back to Lord and Lady Snowshill.

No, they hadn't given their blessing. Not yet anyway. But they would when Winnie secured the hand of the Marquess of Chichester. It was easy enough. Winnie was moderately attractive, from a good family, and came with a reasonable dowry. She had everything to commend her, and Chichester had taken notice almost immediately. At least, that was what society thought. They didn't know all of her secrets.

That was rather the point of secrets. It was best if no one knew just how much she had sinned for if they did, the marquess would never offer for her. The man may have been vile, but he was still of good family and a marquess no less. As long as he thought she had done nothing more than end a previous engagement all would be well. He simply could never know of the rest of it.

No, it needn't matter. She would win him by the end of the season. She was sure of it. It had taken very little to capture his attention. In fact, she had only attended a handful of balls at the beginning of the season to catch his eye. The fact that she had eschewed society for nearly five years had made her sudden reappearance even more alluring, practically pulling the marquess in her direction.

Yes, she would have this all buttoned up by the end of the season.

And then she could begin her punishment.

"I'll say, are those cannons?" Lord Snowshill cried as the band reached a deafening crescendo in their patriotic march. The man took a step forward at the same time he slid a step backward as if bracing himself against the vibrating platform.

His leg struck Winnie's, and as she had already been unbalanced from their earlier collision, she stumbled backward completely, into the group behind them. She muttered apologies that went unheard over the din as she tried to regain her feet.

"It's cannons!" Lord Snowshill sang somewhere behind her, and then an elbow smacked her neatly between the shoulder blades.

Hands pushed at her, shoving her off, which only served to send her farther back into the crowd, separating her from her mother and sister. Finally she planted two feet on the wooden boards and stood up, shoving her bonnet off her forehead where it had come to rest in the melee.

That was when she saw him.

It wasn't possible. Although if she had had any sense left to her, she would have realized he would be there that day. He hadn't seen fighting. The son of a marquess was saved from seeing combat on the Continent by virtue of his title, and as he had been the only heir to the Marquess of Mattingly, his father had ensured he had stayed safely in England.

But he would have come today. He would have stood there just as he was, next to his cousin, Ethan, a man whose face showed exactly what kind of combat he had witnessed.

He would have stood there and remembered, and horribly, she wondered if he thought of her.

Philip.

The name tripped through her mind like a spell that must never be spoken again, and her heart squeezed painfully in her chest.

But through her pain, she became aware of something else. Philip was speaking to Ethan. Animatedly. Almost... angrily.

Whatever was the matter?

But it was at that moment that the trumpet of the band reached its final peak to fall away in an echoing silence of musical triumph, when the cannons stopped firing, when the crowd about them fell into hushed, reverent silence, when Philip's voice was heard by all on the viewing platform.

"Lady Winnaretta Lowe cannot marry the Marquess of Chichester. The man is a bastard of the first order!"

Oh. God.

She was frozen. Frozen to the wooden boards at her feet. Frozen like those posts she had studied so dubiously earlier. They must leave her there, destined to become a part of the viewing platform forever.

But that wasn't what happened. Something far worse occurred.

The crowd's attention turned from the spectacle on the Thames to the man who had shouted such damning words into the silence, but it wasn't only Philip they saw. It was the object of his declaration they saw as well. Because her stumble had placed her not two feet from him.

She could see the muted greens of his eyes, the lines that bracketed his mouth, the ones she had fixated on to steady herself that first time he had kissed her, when the pain of William's death was still raw inside of her, but the reality of her condition had forced her to play a role.

Until she was no longer playacting. Until one day she had *wanted* Philip to kiss her.

And then finally Philip saw her.

Those same beautiful eyes, those green depths from which she had drawn so much comfort, found her with startling accuracy. His expression didn't change as she had thought it would, morphing into surprise and perhaps embarrassment, but she should have known it wouldn't. Instead it hardened, his focus narrowing to her.

She knew that look. It was the look he had given her that last time. The last time he had kissed her when she'd no longer been able to hide the truth of her feelings from him.

It couldn't have gotten worse except just then it did. When the Marques of Chichester stepped from the crowd, his shoulders braced, his lips thinned.

But it was Philip's gaze she held, so she did what she had done five years ago.

She ran.

* * *

PHILIP HODGE, the Earl of Greylock, had learned of the impending marriage of the woman he loved to another man from his cousin and best friend, Ethan D'Arcy, Baron Grays, while standing on a viewing platform overlooking the dedication celebration of Strand Bridge.

"You decided now would be the ideal time to share this piece of news with me?"

His cousin turned his head only the slightest degree to give Philip a curious look. The upturned collar of Ethan's greatcoat nearly hid the scars that marked his face, and for a moment, Philip could almost believe they were boys again, playing at war with wooden swords and toy cannons instead of where they actually were. They stood side by side on a wooden viewing platform, the briny odor of the Thames filling their nostrils as somewhere a band heralded the arrival of a parade of naval vessels that would dedicate the edifice before them as Waterloo Bridge, named for the very same battle that had left its mark on his cousin and best friend.

"I didn't think you would take the news quite like this," Ethan said, his voice never changing, which only served to irk Philip even more. "I thought the decision to end your engagement was an amicable one reached by both parties involved."

"You make it sound like a land deal that went south."

Ethan shrugged and looked away, his gaze wandering over that middle ground of close and far away, so Philip couldn't be sure where his cousin was looking, but the man's casual shrug bothered him. His cousin's words even more.

"Marriage is hardly more than a land deal, isn't it? A contract agreed upon by two people?"

"You're comparing marriage to a land transaction?"

Ethan gave that same careless shrug again. "There's really not much else to it, I'm afraid."

Philip opened his mouth, but his argument died on his lips, momentarily forgetting the devastating news his cousin had just delivered for a much more pressing revelation.

"You don't believe in love." It wasn't a question because somehow Philip understood the truth of it.

Of all the Hodge cousins, Ethan had always been the most stoic, but Philip would never have pegged the man as heartless. The scars on his face were evidence of that. He'd received the wounds that caused them when he'd been searching for his best friend, lost on the field at Waterloo. Ethan hadn't found his friend before the mortar got him, and his friend's body was never recovered. Philip knew Ethan lived with his failure every day. So no, the man was not heartless. But...

"You don't believe in love at all?" Now, when Ethan made no response to his earlier statement, it was a question.

He turned only his head again to eye Philip. His expression gave nothing away though. "Do you believe in love, Philip? Do you think it an emotion or an action?"

Philip gaped. He couldn't help it. He was truly having this conversation now? Here on this platform with cymbals crashing all about him, people pitching their voices to be heard over the din, the roar of cheers coming from the opposite side of the river as spectators cheered the boats on the water.

He swallowed and studied his feet, if only to gather his thoughts. "Love is an emotion, of course. It's something you feel for another person."

Ethan's eyes narrowed the smallest of degrees. "Was it an emotion you felt for Lady Winnaretta?"

Philip had been expecting him to say something else, so when his cousin asked the question, he very nearly replied with the truth.

Yes.

But the weight of that single word caused it to get stuck in his chest, and he instinctively raised his hand to the spot where it had lodged, pain like an echo around his heart.

He was grateful for the pain for it stopped him from saying something he hadn't admitted to anyone except his sister, Caroline, and he knew she would never speak of it. There were those who he thought might suspect, like his dear friend Hawkins Savage, the Earl of Stonegate, but he'd never spoken the words out loud to the man.

He was further saved when the boom of cannons split through the cacophony, overpowering the amalgam of noises that surrounded them. Philip jerked at the sudden sound, but Ethan—God, Ethan. Philip watched it unfold. The way Ethan's gaze swung round, his eyes sharp and wide all at once as though surveying for a threat, his fingers going stiff as his arms came up, reaching for a sword that no longer hung at his side, a musket that no longer swung from his shoulder. But it was Ethan's jaw that Philip watched most closely, afraid his cousin might snap a tooth.

"Hell's teeth," Ethan seethed then, and Philip let out the breath he'd been holding. "What in God's name are they thinking? Cannon fire at the dedication of a war memorial bridge?" He swung his gaze back around, and Philip could see the loathing in his cousin's eyes. "How many men are here today who have heard cannon fire before and feared for their lives?" He looked away again as if he could find the very men who had planned this dedication ceremony.

Not for the first time did Philip feel a stab of guilt. He hadn't heard cannon fire. He hadn't feared for his life at the sound of its magnificent boom. As the only heir to the Marquess of Mattingly, his father had forced him to stay behind, a decision Philip had resisted as best he could, but in the end, his father held control of such decisions.

But then if Philip hadn't remained in England, he never would have been in a position to answer Winnie's plea for help. He never would have met her. He never would have imagined a future with her in it. He never would have had his heart broken.

As soon as the thought entered his mind, he retracted it. He couldn't lament what had happened because if he did, he would be lamenting the greatest thing to have ever happened to him.

Falling in love.

He adjusted his feet against the wooden boards of the platform and refocused on his cousin whose jaw was no longer in danger of snapping clean off. But his eyes remained sharp and guarded.

Philip drew in a deep breath and said the only thing he could think to distract his cousin from his torment. "So who is it that she is to wed?"

He had never been one for masochism, but he would take pain himself if it meant relieving someone he loved of his own torture. Wasn't that how he had gotten into this mess to begin with?

Ethan peered at him for a moment, his vision cloudy. "Who is getting married?"

"Lady Winnaretta." Even her name seemed to get lodged in Philip's throat.

It wasn't even the first time it had come up in recent

weeks, and really, Ethan's news shouldn't have been so star-tling as it was. Not if Philip no longer cared about her anyway. But that was the problem, really. He feared he might always care for Lady Winnaretta Lowe.

"Oh right, the Lowe daughter," Ethan muttered, but his gaze moved away again. "I think she's marrying a marquess."

"A marquess?" He coughed, tugging at his cravat.

Why did he feel a stab of inadequacy at the thought? Shouldn't he wish the best for Winnie? And a marquess. That was rather well done of her.

Chasing that thought came another though, one that had his wandering thoughts stilling with sudden concern. A marquess was quite a catch, but did he make her happy? Did she wish to marry this mysterious marquess or was she being forced into it?

His gaze wandered down to the boats littering the water. Winnie wouldn't be forced into anything. That was some-thing he had respected about her. Even when faced with seemingly insurmountable challenges, she had found a way.

In the end it hadn't mattered though.

"Do you know which marquess?" God in the heavens above, why was he asking? Was there no end to his wish for self-flagellation?

"Which marquess?" Something had captured Ethan's gaze on the other side of the platform.

Philip tried to see, but the path was blocked with any number of bodies, and he couldn't be sure who it was that had caught his cousin's attention.

"The marquess who is marrying Lady Winnaretta?"

Ethan seemed to use a great deal of force to turn his attention back to Philip, and suddenly Philip wished he'd seen who it was that had held his cousin's focus so securely.

"Apparently the man hasn't offered a proposal formally yet. It's merely an understanding."

"An understanding?" Philip didn't care for the spike of protectiveness that surged within him. Hadn't he already given Winnie enough of himself? Why should he still feel this need to protect her? And why so strongly? "The marquess isn't enough of a gentleman to make a straightforward proposal?"

Ethan shook his head. "I'm not sure it's that. The man in question is a great deal older, and only this season has he made it known he was looking for a wife. You know how it is with older gentlemen with specific intentions when it comes to a bride. They practically parade them about as though they were choosing horseflesh."

Philip didn't speak, and eventually Ethan looked over at him, his eyebrows going up.

"It's like that, is it?" Ethan muttered, and Philip could only imagine the expression he wore.

If it even came close to expressing the feelings that warred within him at the idea of Winnie being considered like some kind of prized animal, he was certain his cousin could understand what his words had done.

Ethan held up a hand. "Perhaps not like horseflesh. But you know how it is. These men have certain standards they wish to fulfill. Certain needs." Ethan dropped his hand. "I'm not making this any better. Needless to say, I've heard nothing regarding the gentleman's intentions that would be cause for concern. It's only—" But then Ethan closed his mouth and averted his gaze.

Philip stepped closer, which seemed impossible as they were already crammed onto the viewing platform as it was.

"It's only what?"

Ethan shook his head, but he was at least wise enough to understand Philip was not going to back down. "It's only that the man's business practices have been cause for remark."

"Business practices? What business? The man's a marquess."

Ethan nodded. "That may be, but as you are aware even titled gentlemen are being required to find new avenues of expansion for their titles to remain afloat. It isn't how it used to be when a title could rely on tenants and farming."

"I'm very well aware of the changing economic landscape. What has that to do with Winnie?"

Ethan raised that damned eyebrow again. "Winnie, is it? I don't recall you ever answering my question. Did you love Lady Winnaretta Lowe?"

"Who is the marquess she is to marry, Ethan?" Philip nearly growled in response.

"It's only an understanding, remember. He hasn't officially proposed."

"Ethan."

"The Marquess of Chichester."

The title was a blow to his gut, sending the air straight out of his lungs, so that his response was lodged somewhere in his trachea. It needn't matter for at that moment the band had reached a thundering note, cymbals crashing and drums thumping and trumpets blaring, and he was sure he wouldn't have been able to pluck out the sound of cannon fire in that moment if it really meant it would save his life. He could do nothing but move his jaw uselessly as the title sped through his head.

The Marquess of Chichester. The Marquess of Chichester was despicable. The man conjured shady land dealings and swindled his poor tenants. The man was harmless and terrible all at once, like spoiled milk. If left untouched it wouldn't harm a person but if consumed, it would end in disaster.

Finally Philip found his voice. It was only unfortunate that it was at the same moment everything else went silent.

So when he made his proclamation, everyone on the viewing platform—hell, perhaps everyone as far as Surrey—heard him.

"Lady Winnaretta Lowe cannot marry the Marquess of Chichester. The man is a bastard of the first order!"

The words were already out before he realized what had happened, but it wasn't as though he would retract them anyway. The Marquess of Chichester was a slimy human being, and that was the worst kind. He tricked one into thinking he was innocuous only to take the advantage at the first opportunity.

But none of that mattered, not at all, because as he turned about to take in all the astonished faces gaping in his direction, there was one face that separated itself from the crowd.

Winnie.

She was there.

And she had heard him.

He knew that to be a fact because just at that moment she ran away.

From him.

No, that wasn't it. Chichester had stepped from the crowd too. Philip only gave him a cursory glance because he was already somewhere else.

No, some *when* else, and he was standing, rooted to the ground, his hands holding air where once the woman he loved had stood in his arms, the woman who was then as she was now running away from him.

Only then he had stayed where he was and let her go, committing a mistake that had haunted him for five years. He would not make the same mistake again.

This time when she ran, he went after her.

CHAPTER 2

hy were there so many people here? And why were they all so blurry?

She swiped at her eyes, surprised to find her hand damp with unshed tears. What on earth was she doing crying just then? There was no reason to cry. None at all. It wasn't as though the moment her life had shattered five years ago was playing out again right at that very moment.

In the single beat of her heart she was back there, in the garden of Hodge House. She hadn't known what to do when it had happened. It had taken her so long to realize what *was*, in fact, happening, and her hesitation had allowed for rumors to start. She only knew that because her sister had told her as much. Winnie hadn't been seen in society for nearly a week, but it had taken her that long to adjust to the new reality she faced, to the competing emotions inside of her, the same ones that were swamped by the bone-crushing truth of what had happened.

She'd lost William's baby.

The thought alone, still so sharp after five years, had her stumbling. She caught herself against the facade of the storefront she had managed to reach in her blind run from the viewing platform, and the rough brick scraped her palms through her thin gloves. She welcomed the pain, reveled in it, if only to push the piercing loss of her baby from the front of her mind.

Her baby.

Even now it was so hard to think of the life she had carried as hers alone because when she lost the baby, she'd lost the last of William too. She had thought at the time that she'd never experience such pain again. She had been wrong.

But without the baby, there had been no reason for Philip to save her. She had ended the engagement that night in the garden. Ended it before Philip realized the truth of her sins.

Bodies pressed in around her, and she became aware of a commotion along the street ahead of her. Some sort of procession had reached this side of the bridge, and the crowd gathered shrank in on itself as though to make room. The rough brick that had scraped her palms now pulled at the back of her dress. A man the size of a stout ox stepped back without looking, and she knew what would happen before it did. She was going to be crushed.

Stupidly she held up her arms as if to stop the inevitable, but she was no match for the man's size and girth. She closed her eyes, willing the pain to come if only to flood her mind and push out the memories that haunted her.

But the pain never came.

Something far worse happened instead.

Strong hands seized her at the same time a familiar scent flooded her nostrils. Sandalwood, coffee, and the slightest hint of mint from toothpowder. Her heart stuttered in her chest as though pulled to the scent like a siren call, and she hated herself for it. Hated how she fell into his arms, her knees buckling as she gave herself over to him so easily.

Because she wanted to give herself to him.

She always had, and that was the worst part of her. Her hunger for him, her desire for him, her *love* for him.

She had carried another man's baby while she'd fallen in love with Philip.

William was dead, lost on a forgotten battlefield on the Continent, and she fell in love. She was despicable, disgusting, repulsive, and—

Oh God, he pulled her into his arms, tugging her with him as he turned and slipped through the crowd with an ease she envied. In seconds, she no longer felt the press of bodies around her, their cries of triumph somehow diminished, but she couldn't open her eyes. Not yet. For when she did, she would need to step back and out of his arms, and she didn't know if she could do it again.

"Winnie, are you all right? Were you harmed?"

His voice. The same voice that had soothed her worries, that had whispered endearments to her unborn child, the child that wasn't his but that he had sworn to protect, the same voice that had called to her through the night air of a dark garden.

It was all too much, and finally she forced her eyes open at the same time she commanded her feet to move. It was as though she were learning to walk for the first time, and her knees wobbled in on themselves before she managed to stand. She pressed her palms together, hiding the smudge of brick dust now staining them, and straightened her shoulders.

"Philip." Only his name, and then it was like a potion in her mouth, reviving the past at the same time it conjured a false hope for the future.

She wished that he had looked the same, but horribly, he looked better. The gallant boy who had offered to save her had turned into a striking man, broad of shoulder and strong. Oh God, so strong. She rubbed absently at her arms where he had touched her, forgetting the dust that covered her hands.

"Winnie, I must know if you are all right."

She nodded, the movement haphazard as though her neck had forgotten how to work as well, but she couldn't risk another word. For what would she say?

I loved you?

I love you still?

No, she mustn't. She must get control of herself. Her sister's future depended on it.

"Please let me escort you back to your family. You must see a physician—"

"I can't be seen with you, Philip." The words shot from her mouth, her tone harsh and desperate, so unlike her she startled herself. But it was so much worse when the words came back to her in an echo, and finally she looked up, realizing Philip had dragged her into an alleyway, thick stone walls rising up on either side of them, blocking much of the sunlight but also the world beyond.

She wanted to stay there forever.

She forced herself to look at his face, and for the hundredth time, her heart broke at the sight of him. His lips parted ever so much in shock she knew even he couldn't hide, and she hated herself. Again. Even more.

God, would she never make amends for what she had done?

She held up both hands, gesturing for him to wait as she closed her eyes and tried to regain her composure.

"Philip, I'm sorry. I cannot be seen with you for the sake of my sister's future prospects in society." She spoke each word carefully, enunciating cleanly as she kept her eyes shut. Only when all the words were out did she open them again and focused on his face, his beautiful, familiar face. "She debuted this season, and we are trying ever so hard to secure a match for her. You can understand the pressure she is under. All of us, really, in trying to present her to the greatest advantage."

She wasn't sure what she had been expecting, but the small smile that tipped one side of his mouth was not it.

"Ingrid has had her come out then?"

He remembered her little sister's name. She'd only been a mischievous scamp five years ago during their brief engagement, and yet he had remembered Ingrid's name. Of course he would have.

Winnie nodded. "Yes, she has, and she has a marvelous prospect, but his family is rather cautious. We are all doing our best to convince them of the rightness of this match."

His small smile faltered. "Ingrid is the daughter of an earl, and I'm sure she's grown into a lovely, young woman. Why should her merits ever be in doubt?" He looked away, and she knew he had realized the error of his words.

Winnie was the reason they were doubting. Winnie had ended an engagement and was now the reason her sister might lose the man she loved. Winnie was the reason her sister's only chance at happiness would be stripped from her, and Winnie was the only one who could save it.

"I see," he finally managed.

They stood like that for several seconds, the dull roar of the crowd an awkward overture to the tension that simmered between them. She wanted more than anything to go to him, to feel those strong arms wrap around her once more, to once again believe he had the power to save her. But she had learned long ago that white knights were only found in fairy tales, and that a lady could only depend on herself.

She kept her chin up, her eyes focused on his face, even as his gaze turned more curious rather than caring.

"Winnie, I must apologize for my outburst earlier. I had no intention of disrespecting you like that, and I am sincerely sorry should it cause you or your sister any harm." He swallowed, and for a moment, he appeared almost uncomfortable. "The news of your impending marriage came as rather a shock, I'm afraid, and I reacted poorly."

"It's not impending," she blurted. "He hasn't made a proposal yet." Oh God, why had she just said that?

Because right then she wanted nothing between she and Philip. Not her sister, not Lord and Lady Snowshill, and not the Marquess of Chichester.

Except she couldn't think like that because too much stood between them. Denying it would only hurt them both.

Philip raised an eyebrow. "He hasn't proposed?"

The way he spoke the question made it almost seem as if he already knew the answer, but he wished for her to confirm it.

She shook her head. "No, he hasn't, but we have an understanding of sorts."

Why was she doing this?

She closed her eyes and sucked in a breath. She must get a hold of herself. It was only Philip. He shouldn't matter, except the only thing that had ever mattered was Philip.

She opened her eyes again to find he had stepped closer, so close as to block out the stone walls around them, and she could see only him and the tightness of his features.

"If he hasn't proposed, then you can still end the attachment without harm to your reputation or your sister's. Winnie, you must understand the Marquess of Chichester is not a decent gentleman. He's a swindler and a cheat, and he will—"

"I would ask that you not disparage my future husband." Once again the words sprang from her lips before she realized what she would say, but at Philip's words, some strange defensive reaction had solidified inside of her, roaring up to deflect his intention.

Because she wanted out of it. She wanted out of the entire situation she had created, and Philip's accusations were only more cause to end her pursuit of the marquess. She wanted her sister to marry Robert and be happy, and she wanted—

She wanted Philip.

"I intend to accept his proposal when he should offer it, and I would ask that you not speak of him with such ill intent." She meant not a single word, and so she was surprised by how forcefully they sprang from her lips. But it had to be that way. It must for that was the only way she would convince herself it was the right path. With Philip standing in front of her, it was too easy to forget why she was doing this.

Philip shook his head, his lips parted. "You can't mean that. Winnie, you can't mean to throw away your life like that. Chichester is a scoundrel. He'll treat you as nothing more than chattel."

She wanted to bask in the earnestness that exuded from his eyes. She wanted to lean against him so he could lift this burden from her shoulders. But it was a burden she'd created, and the earnestness in his eyes, that was something she had seen before. That night in the garden when he told her he would marry her anyway, baby or no. And she knew as she did then that Philip Hodge, the Earl of Greylock, was a man of honor, and he would stop at nothing to save her.

So she did something horrible. Again. She preyed on another of his attributes, his infallible respect for others' decisions and feelings.

"Philip, I will marry the Marquess of Chichester because I love him," she lied and watched as, for the second time, she destroyed the man she loved.

* * *

He'd never considered that. Never could have believed it.

Winnie loved him?

The Marquess of Chichester, society's most genteel weasel?

He retracted the thought. Weasels did not deserve such an insulting comparison.

"You love him?" Why was he asking her to repeat the thing that had stopped his heart the first time?

"Yes, I do." She spoke the words so calmly, so assuredly.

It was almost as if they weren't standing alone in an alleyway, a celebration the size of which had not been seen in London in years happening not yards from them. The little sunlight that penetrated that far only served to give him a glimmer of her face, and he couldn't make out her expression clearly.

Was she serious? Did she truly mean what she said?

He shook his head. "Winnie, the marquess is—"

"I think it would be best if we were to address each other by our titles."

His words died on his lips, his brain forgetting how to do…anything. He could only stare, his lips parted, his eyes unblinking.

The only thing that could explain this was simple. This wasn't Winnie. Not the Winnie he had known five years ago. That Winnie had been grieving, hurt, and frightened, and yet the first time he had seen her she had been gathering wildflowers in the fields by her home. He had gone to her as soon as he had received Hawk's letter, begging him to go to her, to help her. Winnie had grown up on the neighboring estate to Hawk's own Stonegate Manor, and it was only natural that she should have sought his help when she realized what had happened.

And it was just as natural that Philip should do his friend's bidding without question. If Hawk thought the girl needed help, then she needed help, and Philip would do all he could to set it to rights. He hadn't known what to expect when he'd ridden up the drive to Oakhurst that afternoon so long ago, but what he hadn't expected was the sight of the solitary woman, standing in the field of wildflowers, her fingertips grazing the swaying blooms. He'd dismounted as quietly as possible, not wishing to break the scene before him, and he'd watched her as he'd approached on foot.

Though she was surrounded by a veritable sea of flowers, only three were in her grasp. She had later explained to him that she had plucked a flower for each of them. One for her, one for the baby, and one for William.

He had offered to marry her on the spot.

But that girl, standing there in the wildflowers, was not the woman who stood before him then. There was something different about her now, something he couldn't quite name. But it was edgy and hard, and worst of all, calculated. What had happened to Winnie?

Had it been too much? Had the grief of losing William and then the baby done this to her? Was that why she had fallen in love with a scoundrel like Chichester?

Suddenly he believed her. Suddenly it was too *easy* to believe her.

Everything inside of him stopped at once, and it was like time itself had splintered around him. There was what he had believed up until that point, and then what was quickly becoming the reality of what it truly was.

He had thought Winnie broken and weeping for what might have happened. Devastated for the baby she would never have, of the life they would never lead, and the very thought of it had been his own aching burden to carry these past five years, but that wasn't it at all.

She had closed herself off from the hurt. She must have if she thought herself in love with Chichester now.

"I see," he finally said, words coming more easily now. He took a step back. "I wish you both much happiness then."

Was it a trick of the half-light or did she flinch at his words?

"Thank you, my lord." Her words were dry and unfeeling.

"If I may not escort you back to your family, may I at least follow at a distance to ensure your safety?"

She shifted, and a shaft of sunlight lit her face for a moment. He was taken back there, to that field of wildflowers, and for an instant she was the same girl again, broken and grieving and still trying to find happiness among the ashes.

For some absurd reason, he took a step closer to her. "I shouldn't wish anything to happen to you, Lady Winnaretta, and the crowd seems to be growing more fervent in their celebrating."

Her gaze traveled behind him as if taking in the crowds they had just escaped.

"I think that is probably wise." She licked her lips, and he wondered briefly if he were making her nervous.

He stepped to the side and gestured for her to make her way toward the street, but she hesitated, and in that hesitation, he poured every hope and doubt he'd been harboring.

For he was harboring them. Something just wasn't right about this whole thing.

He had pictured seeing Winnie again. Of course he had. He'd dreamt of it. He'd practiced what he might say to her, wondered what she might say to him. He couldn't even recall the number of times he had stopped himself from trying to contact her then, from trying to change her mind, to not call off their engagement because the temptation had been far too great and often.

But he hadn't done it because God damn him, his back-bone was built entirely of respect for others.

If Winnie wished to end their engagement and begged for him to leave her be, then he'd done it.

Until now.

This wasn't even his fault really. How was he to know she would be standing feet away when he made an absolute ass of himself?

"Lady Winnaretta." Her formal name stuck in his mouth like too much fudge. "May I ask you something?"

She had picked up her skirts as if to make her way over the uneven cobblestones of the alley, but she paused now, lifting only her gaze to him. She blinked once, and he took that as an affirmation.

"How is it that you became acquainted with the Marquess of Chichester?"

She must have shifted in her attempt to gather her skirts because when she lifted her face to him, he could see her expression now lit by a beam of sunlight. He saw the moment hesitation tripped across her face at his question.

"Became acquainted with him? I'm not sure I understand. His lordship is a prominent member of society. Everyone knows of him."

"Yes, everyone does, but how is it that you became the center of his attention?" Her eyes narrowed just the slightest bit in suspicion, and he rushed on. "It's just that although I may find Chichester's character to be less than noteworthy, he is still a marquess, and as it's been mentioned, it's rather an advantage to have his attentions."

Something passed over her eyes then, something hard and dark, and she said, "Do you think I'm unworthy of a marquess, my lord?"

He shook his head quickly. "Not at all, Lady Winnaretta. I would never suggest such a thing." How ridiculous was this? The clunkiness of their titles taking up the space between them until they could do nothing more than stand farther apart to accommodate them. "It's only that, well…might I be frank with you, my lady?"

She dropped her skirts now and crossed her arms over her chest. "Am I going to be able to stop you?"

"I would think not." He couldn't stop a small grin at this brief glimpse of the Winnie he had known. "Lady Winnaretta, the last time I saw you, you were not a whole person, understandably so. Grief had taken its toll on you, and I very much hated watching it strip you of the light I knew you carried inside of you. My only hope was that one day you would find the love that you so deserved, and that the tale would be one filled with sunshine and happiness, so much so that it would forever dispel the sadness that threatened to drown you in those dark times." He stopped when her lips separated ever so slightly, and he watched her eyes wander unblinkingly over his face. He pressed on. "I remain hopeful, Lady Winnaretta. Please tell me yours is a tale worthy of my wish for you." It was the truth at the heart of it, except when he'd thought of her finding happiness, he'd always dreamt it would be with him.

She took a step back and pressed a hand to her stomach. "Oh. I see. You—" She licked her lips, looked down and back up again. "You…that is to say, I—" She stopped again and shook her head. "Your kindness flatters me, my lord."

He tilted his head. "It isn't kindness, Lady Winnaretta. It is simple fact. I've never met someone more deserving of happiness than you." He thought she wouldn't be more surprised if he'd slapped her in the face.

Her eyes went wide, and her lips remained parted for several seconds before she said, "Thank you, my lord, but I assure you it is no grand tale of love that I have to tell you. I'm afraid it's all rather ordinary."

She lifted her hand, and her fingers collided with the brim of her bonnet absently. She pulled her hand back, tucking it into the palm of the other as though she may have forgotten she wore a hat and had meant to push her hair back. She had often done that, he remembered, and he wondered how terribly flustered he'd made her. All the better to get the truth from her.

"The marquess and I were introduced through mutual acquaintances, and I'm sorry to say the rest progressed as usual." She smiled, but the corners of her mouth wavered as though she weren't entirely sure he had taken the bait.

He hadn't, but she needn't know that. "I see. So it was the usual then? Promenades? Rides in the park? Tell me, Lady Winnaretta, has the marquess been…" He had let his voice drop, and now he simply let it hang there on his last word as she tipped nearer to him, so close he could smell the lavender of her soap, and memories threatened to suffocate him. But he managed to finish with, "filling your dance card?"

She jerked back and made that aborted gesture with her hand again. She tucked it more firmly against her chest with the opposite hand. "Yes, he has, in fact." Now when she smiled it was entirely unsure, and he thought spots of color may have come to her cheeks. "One can hardly blame him though. Marriage is an awfully big step, and I'm sure he wishes to know I am suited to the task."

"Of marriage?" He let one eyebrow drift up. "Trust me when I say you're more than suited to it, Lady Winnaretta." He snared her gaze with his and refused to look away.

He could feel the tension mounting like the flames in a hearth, growing higher and hotter with every passing second as the fire consumed the fuel meant to drive it into a frenzy.

Winnie took a step back so swiftly she nearly collided with the stone wall behind her. He caught her elbow delicately but never closed the distance between them, not even by an inch. He stood the perfect gentleman at a discreet distance, politely holding a lady's arm who appeared to have encountered such duress. Then he smiled, diabolically, and he watched as her lips thinned in obvious annoyance.

If this was the game she wished to play, she would see just how good he was at it.

"My lady, please, allow me to help you. These cobblestones can be hazardous."

She didn't speak another word. She simply turned, tugged her elbow free, and made her way back to the street. He watched her go, keeping a discreet but close distance behind her.

Never once had he gone against his morals when it came to the decisions of others. He respected the choices that other people made. Hell, he even respected his younger sister's decisions even when he knew she played with danger. Did she really think he hadn't noticed how much time she spent with Hawk as of late? Philip only hoped his friend would act the gentleman in the end.

No, he never overstepped his bounds. Not until now.

But now, he had no choice.

He must stop Lady Winnaretta Lowe's engagement.

CHAPTER 3

"I'm sure not everyone in London heard him," Ingrid said, poking her needle awkwardly through the linen handkerchief in her hand so that it stabbed her in the finger. Again.

Winnie placed her hands gently over her sister's to still them. They were seated by the front windows to capture the best light as they once more went over embroidery, not a strong subject for Ingrid. In fact, Winnie was finding it difficult to find a subject that was for Ingrid.

"You must understand where your needle shall travel before you place the stitch," she said calmly, both because she didn't wish to scold her sister for something so silly as a slipped stitch, but also because her sister still held the needle and after weeks of trying to get Ingrid to learn how to properly place a stitch, her sister was unfortunately still far too dangerous with the small implement. She held her sister's hands between her own and mimicked a properly placed stitch before releasing her grip to allow her sister to make the stitch again. "Besides," she continued, placing her hands in her lap, "it shouldn't matter anyway. It's not as though

Lord Greylock's opinion is so highly regarded in society." She shrugged as though to convince her sister of her words when Winnie knew perfectly well she was attempting to convince herself. "He isn't even the marquess yet. He still holds his father's lesser title. Why would anyone pay attention to him?"

Her father spoke up from his position in the bay window where he was tinkering with his funicular railway model. "I pay attention to him. I've always liked Greylock. Sound head on his shoulders."

Winnie chose to ignore this.

"Dear heavens, it's made the scandal sheets," her mother breathed from her perch beside her husband, a plate of saffron buns at her elbow, the morning's newspapers stacked haphazardly about her, a scandal sheet gripped between both hands.

Winnie could not ignore this.

"What's made the scandal sheets?" Ingrid asked, her fingers frozen on the handkerchief as Winnie hoped her heart would not beat directly out of her chest to go parading about the drawing room. Not for the first time did Winnie wonder if her mother's habit of consuming all and any news weren't more dangerous than it was beneficial.

What looked like indolent behavior between the plate of saffron buns and the scandal sheets was actually her mother's greatest weapon. Ada Lowe, the Countess of Bibury, knew absolutely everything that happened in London and sometimes even beyond. There was no bit of news that she found beneath her, and so sometimes she knew when a marriage was on the verge of disaster before the wedded couple did. She knew when debutantes were tarnished, when business deals were struck, and when opportunities were created within a void. Lady Bibury was a walking encyclopedia of present-day knowledge. And it was all thanks to her desire for a quiet morning of reflection to start her day.

Winnie focused on the saffron buns to keep her mind from jumping to the very thing she knew her mother must have found among her scandal sheets.

"It's in *Mrs. Woodbridge's Whispers*. Heavens to St. Christopher, she's quoted him exactly!" Her mother shoved the last bite of a bun into her mouth.

"Who has she quoted exactly?" Ingrid asked.

Mother shook her head as she contemplatively chewed, her eyes roaming over the page held before her.

Winnie stood, unable to bear it any longer, and went to her mother, perching on the arm of the sofa to read over her mother's shoulder. Ingrid followed, the handkerchief discarded on the chair where she'd sat beside Winnie. Her father continued to wind the strings that served as cables in his model, either oblivious or uninterested. Winnie suspected it was the latter.

Their mother poked at the scandal sheet with a buttery finger, and Winnie found the place in a neat one-inch column of text.

SPECTATORS AT YESTERDAY's Waterloo Bridge dedication got more than a show of military power. Philip Hodge, the Earl of Greylock, chose yesterday's celebrated event to declare a sentiment this author thinks the gentleman meant to keep private. Dare I repeat it here? Or rather, must I? It's this author's impression that everyone in London heard his lordship's proclamation. It would have been impossible not to. But for those who have the unfortunate circumstance of not having heard, here is what the earl said:

. . .

"Lady Winnaretta Lowe cannot marry the Marquess of Chichester. The man is a bastard of the first order!"

I am nothing if not fair, and should the Marquess of Chichester have a reply, I should be happy to print it.

Winnie straightened, backing into the bust of Leonardo da Vinci her father had sculpted in an uncommon flourish of artistic release. She grabbed da Vinci's head to steady both it and herself and stood pressed against the wall.

"She did quote him," she breathed.

Ingrid straightened. "I'm so sorry, sister, but I must retract my earlier statement. If everyone in London hadn't heard him before, they at least know what he said now." She gestured weakly at the scandal sheet their mother now held close to her face as though that might change what it said.

"Oh Winnie, I'm afraid this will not do. What will the marquess think?" Mother sat up, deftly moving the piles of newspapers around her. "You know how important it is to secure the marquess's proposal." The woman's eyes drifted to Ingrid who stood perfectly still except for her hands, which she wrung together in obvious anguish, and her father—lud, her father had even looked up from his model and pinned her with a hard look that gave her more questions than answers.

Winnie's heart clenched, her mind going blank except for one terrible thought. The Marquess of Chichester had not gone after her the previous day. Only Philip had. When she had returned to her family, it was to find the marquess had left with the gentlemen he had been in conversation with to retire to his club. She didn't expect him to care about her, but it would have made things easier if he didn't behave like the scoundrel Philip had called him. Well, Philip had called him something else, but scoundrel would do.

She released da Vinci's head and took a resolute step into the room. "This will not get beyond our control. It wasn't me who spoke the words, and I can state that as a matter of fact to the marquess, should he voice concern." She stopped at the replica of the Pantheon that stood on the sideboard opposite the windows and turned about. "There is no reason for him to doubt his intentions." She paused, letting her thoughts catch up to her before pushing away from the sideboard. "Lady Satterwhite's garden party is the day after tomorrow. Anyone who is anyone will be there, including Chichester." She'd reached the other side of the room and spun about to face her mother and little sister. "I shall speak to the marquess there and assure him I do not share Lord Grey-lock's viewpoint." She smiled and caught it before it wobbled. "See. There is nothing at all to cause concern."

"My ladies and your lordship."

The three of them jumped at the soft, docile tones of their butler, Akers, while her father remained fixated on adjusting one of the strings. It was Winnie who recovered first and turned to find the servant in the doorway. Akers was a man of middling years who was slim of stature except for a generous paunch, evidence of his affair with Cook's mince-meat pies.

"Yes, Akers, what is it?"

Akers bowed ever so slightly as he said, "The Earl of Greylock is here to see Lady Winnaretta."

Only then did Winnie's eyes take in the silver salver with its single calling card lying atop it.

She heard her mother's gasp and Ingrid's whispered, "Oh no," but it all disappeared into the ocean that roared suddenly in Winnie's ears. She had made a mistake. She had thought to rely on Philip's inability to go against a person's wishes when she should have remembered Philip's far more troublesome quality.

His need to help.

He knew perfectly well the unsavory character that was the Marquess of Chichester, and he was clearly not going to give up. A flash of memories flew through her mind then. Philip standing in the garden that night, the white of his shirt matching the white of his teeth as he smiled in the near dark, as he opened his arms to her. Philip as he was the day before, still in the shadows, still reaching for her.

"Please have Mathilda see to him." The words shot from her mouth like a sentencing.

"Winnie, no," her mother exclaimed, getting to her feet, the scandal sheet falling to the floor forgotten.

"Winnie, you can't," Ingrid said, taking an aborted step forward, her hands hanging in the air as if she had been about to plead.

Winnie looked directly at Akers. "Yes, please have Mathilda see to him, Akers."

But even the butler hesitated, his lips quivering as if in concern before he said, "Mathilda, my lady? Are you certain?"

Winnie nodded once. "Yes, Mathilda. Thank you, Akers." She turned away before she could change her mind. Forcing Philip to face Mathilda, Winnie's beloved nurse then nanny and now maid, was the cruelest thing she'd ever done. Mathilda's family had been serving Winnie's mother's family for generations, their roots solidly aligned with her maternal family's lines in Denmark-Norway, and such longevity had created a fierce and unwavering loyalty in the woman. Winnie almost felt sorry for Philip.

Almost.

She stood before her mother and sister, hands raised in supplication. "I'm sure Mathilda will be gentle with him."

Ingrid scoffed. "When has Mathilda ever been gentle?" She took a sharp step forward. "Does she know it was you who ended the engagement?"

Winnie opened her mouth to assure her sister that she had told Mathilda the truth, but then she snapped her lips shut, a foreboding sense of dread creeping over her like a fog.

"Winnie?" This was her mother who had stepped up to her, gripping Winnie's upper arm in one strong hand.

Winnie looked up in her mother's face, pinched with concern. Though Winnie was tall, she wasn't as tall as her statuesque mother whose Scandinavian roots showed in her compelling height and white-blonde hair. Once, Winnie had envied her sister for getting their mother's coloring, the commanding bearing their height demanded. Winnie had the misfortune of getting her father's coloring, nondescript brown hair and brown eyes best suited for blending in with the wallpaper.

Winnie didn't mind so much now, not when she had so much to hide.

"I can't remember what I told her," Winnie whispered, unable to even look in Ingrid's direction.

"Oh Lucifer, she's going to kill the man," their mother said, but Ingrid was already moving for the door.

"I'm sure everything will be all right," Father reassured everyone, his face still buried in his model.

Akers appeared again, his poof of gray-speckled hair flying about his forehead as if he were running. "Lord and Lady Snowshill," he cried just before the people in question strode into the room.

Winnie's chest tightened in immediate apprehension.

Lady Snowshill hadn't even removed her hat and gloves at the door, and her fists clenched around folds of her skirt as though she'd been in a hurry to get to the drawing room. There was also the look of sheer menace on the woman's angular face that had Winnie straightening just as Akers mumbled, "And their son, the Honorable Mr. Clarke."

Robert came through the door, his smile like a literal ray of sunshine banishing the darkness that had flooded the room. He tore between both of his parents to Ingrid, his hands outstretched for hers.

"Lady Ingrid," he said, his voice familiar and warm, and Winnie watched as her sister's concern for Philip disappeared, already forgotten when Robert's hands touched hers.

Winnie allowed herself a moment of happiness, watching her sister's smile bloom at seeing Robert, before turning to Lady Snowshill.

"Lady—" Winnie began, but Lady Snowshill cut her off.

"Was that the Earl of Greylock we saw leaving?"

Oh well, it seemed Philip had survived his encounter with Mathilda. That was some relief. Unless Mathilda had simply tucked the man's dead body into his carriage and sent him back to Hodge House. Lud, what an awful idea.

Winnie shook her head, as much to clear her thoughts as to answer Lady Snowshill. "I'm terribly sorry, Lady Snowshill, I don't know of what you speak."

"We have not seen the Earl of Greylock today, my lady." Winnie's mother came over to them, her hands lifted in supplication, and Winnie couldn't help but admire the woman's way with words.

Technically they hadn't seen Philip, but that didn't mean he hadn't called.

"I saw him leaving when we pulled up. The carriage bore the Hodge family crest. I saw it." Lady Snowshill was practically spitting now, her crepey jowls jiggling with each word.

"Lady Snowshill, please." Winnie started at her father's deep voice, having almost forgotten the man was there. "You mustn't vex yourself. Lord Greylock has not been in this room today, and you mustn't upset yourself so." He said all of this while not looking up from his model once.

When Winnie turned back to the Clarkes, it was to find twin expressions of curiosity tinged with something else—was it concern?—on the faces of Lord and Lady Snowshill.

Winnie forced a smile and made her way over to the chairs by the front windows. "Please, Lady Snowshill, sit, and I shall ring for tea."

The woman stomped over to the chair and sat with an emphatic flourish as if doing so out of spite. Winnie hadn't even made it to the bell pull in the corner when the woman let out a cry of pain and sprang from the chair. Ingrid swung about as their mother surged forward. Winnie stood suspended, one hand on Leonardo da Vinci's head as she leaned over to grasp the bell pull.

"Lady Snowshill, whatever is the matter?" Ingrid said, her voice soft with concern.

The woman didn't reply. She didn't need to because in her hand was Ingrid's discarded embroidery, the afternoon sun glinting sharply off the needle still stuck in it.

Ingrid's eyes flew to Winnie, and in them, she saw an ocean of pleading. Winnie patted old Leonardo on the head and swept across the room, snatching the needlework from Lady Snowshill.

"I'm terribly sorry, Lady Snowshill," she said once again, her voice perfectly even. "I'm always leaving my things lying about." She gave her sister a pointed look.

Winnie would see this thing through, but it wasn't as though she couldn't do with a little help.

* * *

"What do you know about breaking up engagements?"

Hawkins Savage, the Earl of Stonegate, looked up from his drink. "Why are you asking me this?"

Philip dropped into the chair beside his friend and raised a hand to the passing footman, who recognized Philip and nodded before scurrying off. Philip tossed his gloves aside and settled in. The club wasn't so busy at this time in the afternoon, and if the morning's events were of any indication, he was going to need help in his plan.

"Because I need to break up an engagement. I thought that would be obvious from the question."

Hawk eyed him over his glass. "But why are you asking me? This sounds like something for Ethan to handle."

Philip shook his head. "We all know Ethan is far too straitlaced for such things. I really need someone with a more malleable moral character."

Hawk's face didn't change as he said, "You have always showered me with praise, Philip. I think that's why we're such dear friends."

Philip only smiled. Hawk sat up, dropping his glass to the table between their chairs, and Philip noted the dark patches beneath his friend's eyes.

"Are you not sleeping well?"

Hawk nearly bobbled his glass, catching it at the last moment before it careened off the side of the table. He didn't look up as he said, "Why would you ask that?"

Philip didn't miss the note of suspicion in his voice and wondered not for the first time what was going on between his best friend and his sister. Caroline hated Hawk, had done for years. She blamed Hawk for what had transpired between Philip and Winnie, namely the aborted engagement and what she called the near ruination that followed. Hawk, being too much of a gentleman, had never corrected Caroline's beliefs that Philip was the one to cause the need for an engagement, and Philip wouldn't tell Winnie's secrets. It had left them all in a bit of a mire, but Philip respected Winnie too damn much to tell anyone of her past, even his own sister.

"You look as though you've been trampled by a runaway cart. Has Caroline been tormenting you more than usual?"

Hawk choked and tried to cover it with a cough as he tugged at his cravat. "It's nothing I can't handle," he said, but Philip didn't miss how his friend had avoided answering the question. "Now then, what's this about ending an engagement?"

The footman arrived then and set down two fresh glasses and a decanter of dark liquid, sweeping Hawk's empty glass from the table in a single smooth motion.

Philip took the break in conversation to study his friend, wondering at the man's obvious discomfort. Philip had left for school at a tender age and was gone with much regularity from the family home for most of fifteen years. His Grand Tour had been delayed because of the war, and then everything with Winnie had occurred.

By the time Philip had resurfaced, once more residing at Hodge House, he realized much had changed since he'd left when a boy, and his sister, Caroline's behavior was evidence of it. But there was more to it than his sister simply being concerned for the scandal his engagement could have caused if anyone outside the family had learned why he was marrying Winnie. Caroline's intent was more frantic than that, and not for the first time did Philip feel a pang of guilt for abandoning his sister in the maelstrom that had become their parents' marriage.

Philip waited until the footman was out of earshot before he said, "I've just learned Lady Winnaretta Lowe is to marry the Marquess of Chichester."

"You're joking." Hawk's voice was flat.

"I'm afraid not." Philip poured for both of them and handed Hawk his glass.

"Creedmoor?" Hawk asked, using the marquess's family name. "She's to marry Creedmoor? How do you know this?"

"Ethan actually." Philip paused to take a restorative sip of his drink. "But I confirmed it with Lady Winnaretta herself."

Hawk sat forward, turning fully in his chair to face Philip. "You spoke to Winnie?" His friend's voice had dropped to a near whisper, his eyes intense as he awaited Philip's answer.

Philip nodded as he waited for the lump in his throat to dissipate. Winnie had been like a specter between them for five years. It was Hawk who had orchestrated their meeting, and without his involvement, Philip may never have met Winnaretta Lowe. Philip wasn't sure of Hawk's feelings on the subject as the two had never spoken of it, but Philip suspected Hawk knew what Winnie had come to mean to him.

"I did, but it did not go as I had imagined it would."

Hawk gripped the arm of his chair. "What happened? Were you alone? How? Where was I?"

Philip frowned. "You're beginning to sound like my sister." He watched Hawk visibly swallow and decided to give his friend a reprieve. "It was at the Waterloo Bridge dedication. I may have inadvertently mentioned something that was not for others to hear."

Hawk leaned back with a low whistle. "So you did proclaim to everyone that she shouldn't marry Chichester. I thought those scandal sheets were full of nonsense."

"You read scandal sheets?"

Hawk gave a one-shoulder shrug. "Grandmother does. She was practically interested in that bit. Asked me herself if it were true."

Hawk had been raised by his grandmother after his parents were killed in a carriage accident when he was very young.

"Lady Sherrill's heard of my latest scandal? She's in Surrey."

Again, Hawk gave a half shrug. "What can I say? Scandal is speedier than you might think. I received her letter just this morning, asking if it were true."

Philip shook his head. It needn't matter who had heard of his gaff. It only mattered that he act now.

He leaned forward, replacing his glass on the table. "I must stop it, Hawk. I can't let Winnie marry a bastard like Creedmoor."

"What happened when you spoke to her? Did she tell you why she agreed to marry him?"

Philip's mind went back to the alleyway, and he could picture her so clearly, the sunlight falling across her face so he could only see her in pieces. "She said she loves him."

"No." Hawk spoke the single word without inflection or emphasis as though he were dismissing someone's insistence that the world was flat.

"I'm afraid so."

Hawk shook his head. "It's not possible. Are we speaking of the same Winnie? She would never agree to marry a man like Creedmoor."

Philip held up his hands. "She said she's in love, and she said we can't be seen together. It will damage Lady Ingrid's prospects in society."

Hawk raised an eyebrow. "Ingrid's come out then? Isn't she too young?"

"Apparently not." It was Philip's turn to shrug.

Hawk sat back. "This doesn't seem right. Lady Winnaretta marrying the Marquess of Chichester and telling you to stay away from her." He'd been studying the air in front of his nose, but he turned to look at Philip then. "Does something seem wrong to you?"

"It does," he said, picking up his drink once more. "And I intend to stop it."

Hawk grinned. "You intend to save her? Again?"

Philip set down his glass and made sure he held Hawk's gaze as he said, "I will always save her."

There was a beat of silence then as the weight of five years pressed down on them, and in that space, everything that they hadn't said to each other passed wordlessly between them. Hawk's letter from the Continent asking Philip to marry Winnie, Philip traveling to Surrey to find Winnie, the engagement, the heartache, the joy, and the devastation. It was all there, said and unsaid.

"What are you planning to do?" Hawk said, and Philip knew his friend understood it all.

"I agreed with her," he said, taking another sip.

"You did what?"

"I agreed with her," Philip repeated. He could still see her as though she were standing before him, asking him to use their titles as though calling her something else would make his heart forget who she was.

"Agreed with her about what exactly?" Hawk pressed.

"She asked that I not be seen with her in public, and that I address her as Lady Winnaretta."

"That's not Winnie."

Philip nodded. "I know, and I must find out what's really going on here."

Hawk shook his head. "How do you plan to do that? You recall what it was like to end an engagement. I'm not certain Winnie will survive another scandal like that."

Philip was already shaking his head. "Their engagement isn't formal. There's only an understanding between them."

Both of Hawk's eyebrows rose. "An understanding?" He made a derisive noise. "Coward. He can't properly ask for a betrothal either? The man is a bastard." He shook his head.

"And Winnie claims to love him? Even without a proper proposal?"

"That's what she said."

"Do you believe her?"

Philip thought back to their encounter, about what had happened before they had spoken. It was like her body had remembered him. When he'd reached her in the crowd, her body had turned to his, melding herself against him. He'd felt it. Every one of her muscles in turn had gone slack, her shoulders curling into him. It was as if she had remembered where she'd belonged.

And then she'd stepped back, and the spell was broken.

"I don't believe her." He hadn't meant to whisper the words, but he was still lost in that single moment. That one second when he had thought his very dreams were coming to reality.

Hawk shook his head and picked up his glass. "You've got a difficult road ahead of you, mate."

Philip tensed. "I know. I tried to call on her this morning."

This time there was real fear in Hawk's eyes as he said, "Mathilda?"

Philip nodded gravely. "I only just survived with my life."

"Fists?"

"She carried me bodily from the house."

Hawk raised both eyebrows again. "She didn't."

Philip tugged at his cravat, the emasculating episode still painfully fresh. "I'm afraid she did. I was standing there on the front step waiting for the butler to return when the door opened, and Mathilda came barreling out." He shook his head. "I didn't stand a chance."

Hawk sucked in a breath. "Oh mate. I wasn't even referring to the physical aspect of this plot of yours. I was speaking of the other stuff."

"What other stuff? If Winnie doesn't really love him, then

I only need to convince her there's another way out of whatever mess she thinks she's gotten into."

Hawk shook his head again. "That's not the issue though, is it? If she doesn't really love Chichester, she's going to do everything she can to convince you of it because, really, she's trying to convince herself."

"You're saying she will stubbornly defend the falsehood?"

"Of course she will." Hawk tapped the arm of his chair with one finger. "She will not admit to you what she won't admit to herself. You're never going to convince her of the wrongness of such a match."

"But we have a shared history. I know things about her that Chichester doesn't. I can leverage that knowledge—"

"Did her parents know why you suddenly asked to marry her five years ago?"

This stopped Philip instantly. He remembered his introduction to Lord and Lady Bibury that terribly bright day in Surrey. Only then they had still been Mr. and Mrs. Lowe. Lord Bibury hadn't unexpectedly inherited the title yet. Mr. Lowe was a great bear of a man with layers of mustaches and gray hair unfashionably long. His cuffs had been stained with ink, his fingers carrying a telltale dusting of dried clay as then the man had always been tinkering in his workshop, making models of one kind or another. Mrs. Lowe was not much different, only with her height came an unparalleled grace, and on her fingers, butter and newspaper ink.

Then, it hadn't been so unusual that the son of a marquess should ask for their elder daughter's hand in marriage. But now she was the daughter of an earl, and he felt a sharp pang at thinking how she deserved to be a marchioness one day.

"Yes, her parents did know," he said finally.

He had braced himself on the whole of the journey to Surrey, not knowing what sort of confrontation he might find there, but what he found instead was no confrontation at all. Winnie's parents were generous and understanding. If anything, Mr. Lowe had badgered Philip about his decision, asking him if he was certain he wished to raise another man's child. It was the one question he hadn't thought about on the way to Surrey, too wrapped up in the urgency of Hawk's letter to think of much beyond getting there. But when he'd seen Winnie standing there in the sea of wildflowers, their stems swaying with the touch of her hand as though she held the power to bend nature itself, he knew the answer without hesitation.

Yes.

It would always be a *yes* when it came to Winnie.

Hawk leaned closer. "So if Winnie has already broken one of society's most unforgiving rules, what is it she's done that is so reprehensible as to deserve to be married to the Marquess of Chichester for the rest of her life?"

For the first time since the idea came into his head, Philip's mind went utterly blank at Hawk's declaration. "You're saying Winnie thinks she deserves to marry the marquess? That she's doing it as some sort of punishment?"

Hawk nodded. "You'll never convince her to end it. She thinks it's something that must be done."

"Then what is it I'm to do?"

Hawk's smile was painfully understanding. "You must convince the Marquess of Chichester to end it."

"The marquess?" Philip shook his head. "I will have no association with the man. How am I to..." He let his voice trail off as Hawk nodded.

"You will have an association with the man, I'm afraid. You will even be his friend. And as his friend, you will convince him that marrying Winnaretta Lowe is the last thing he should do."

Philip blinked. "I knew I came to the right man."

Hawk sat back, wrinkling his nose. "I'm not sure if that's a compliment."

CHAPTER 4

She spotted Chichester almost immediately.

She took a step forward, so intent on her need to fix this blunder that the scandal sheets were only too happy to amplify, that for a moment she thought she was seeing Philip where Chichester stood. She halted, her elbow jostling a topiary of what might have been a rendering of Puck. She cupped her elbow and eyed the menacing thing.

What was the matter with her? Philip was not lying in wait at every turn. He had not returned to the house since the day she'd sent Mathilda after him, and Winnie thought he might finally be obeying her wishes. She hadn't asked Mathilda what she had said to him to have him leaving so adroitly, and Mathilda hadn't offered. The woman was more effective than a brick wall at keeping Winnie closed off from the outside world.

She felt a chill pass over her at the thought. Even as she stood there in Lady Satterwhite's garden, surrounded by society's finest, laughter and conversation filling the air, sunshine warming her shoulders, she felt utterly alone. As she watched Chichester converse with a group of gentlemen, she couldn't help but think of the first time she'd seen Philip.

He'd looked like a knight errant.

He'd been atop his horse, and it was likely just a trick of perspective that made him appear so dashing, as though he were coming to save her from all the things that could hurt her.

She hadn't even realized she'd wandered as far as the wildflowers at the edge of the park of the cottage they had rented that summer at Oakhurst. She had held three stems in her hands before she knew what she was doing, and for a moment, she felt a pang of sadness for that Winnie. She'd been so lost.

No one had informed her of William's death. There hadn't been reason to think she should have been informed. No one knew of what they had done before he'd left for the Continent, or what had happened because of it. They thought her a girl he had only danced with once at a country assembly. They couldn't know…

She heard of William's death in passing at the conclusion of the church service the previous Sunday. It was spoken of so casually in hushed whispers of reverence that Winnie had blurted out her disbelief and asked the gossiping matrons to repeat what they'd just said.

She couldn't remember anything after that. The next she knew she was waking up in her bed at the cottage, her mother holding her hand. The grief must have overwhelmed her, and she'd fainted away. She told her mother everything then. For one blessed moment, Winnie had actually believed her mother could fix it. Ada Lowe could fix anything. At least, that was what Winnie had believed once. But Ada Lowe couldn't fix this.

She gathered herself, and at a much more leisurely pace, made certain she entered Chichester's line of vision as she pretended to peruse the topiaries lining the terrace. Next to Puck there was a Hera and a Zeus and strangely enough a Poseidon. She lost track after that as she kept one eye trained on Chichester as she slipped directly before him.

She wore her new walking gown in the palest of lavenders, and she knew it set off her dark hair to its advantage. She'd had Mathilda style it in a cascade of curls to one side of her head, so it fell like a waterfall underneath her bonnet. The curls would never hold. Winnie's hair was too straight for it, but right then, she knew she looked her best, and she must catch Chichester's eye immediately.

But the dratted man kept talking.

If anything he grew more animated in his discussion and even began to gesticulate as if his words weren't enough. Heavy brow fell into a straight line as he concentrated, his face dappled in the shadows of his beaver hat.

She frowned but only for a second. Chichester couldn't catch her with such a look on her face. Gad, what would he think?

"I wonder. Is he conversing with those gentlemen, or are they playing a game of charades?"

Winnie jumped, and this time she all but knocked the topiary behind her clean from its pot. It was caught by the gentleman who had startled her though, and the thing was saved from utter ruin and in turn, Winnie as well. She wasn't going to thank the gentleman, however. Certainly not. Because she knew that voice. It was the same one that haunted her dreams.

"I told you to stay away from me."

Philip raised a single eyebrow, an eyebrow she was coming to find very annoying. "Ah, but you didn't."

"Yes, I did." She was nearly hissing now.

"No, you didn't. I recall exactly what you said to me, and you didn't ask me to stay away from you. If you had, I would have honored such a request." He pressed a hand to his chest. "You know I am nothing if not honorable, Lady Winnaretta."

She forgot that she was trying to maintain a pleasant expression and simply scowled. "I did make such a request. You will not fool me, Lord Greylock."

He held up a finger then, and she suddenly wished to break it. "You said we couldn't be seen together, and to that, I wholeheartedly agreed."

She looked about them to check if the world had suddenly tilted off its axis. "Then what are you doing here?"

He at least withdrew the finger. "I agreed that we shouldn't be seen then. It would have been terrible for your reputation. But you didn't say anything about future occurrences. I am here today for you actually."

She snapped her mouth shut on what she'd been about to say and pressed a hand to her stomach. She could not allow this man to get the better of her and keep her from her intentions. She closed her eyes and wished for patience as she said, "And just what exactly has compelled you to such a notion?"

"Guilt."

The single word had her eyes flying open, and finally she let herself look at him directly. Her heart thudded as if in recognition, as if it knew that square jaw, those warm green eyes.

"What do you mean guilt?" Her voice had lost its edge of defense and was now soft with apprehension.

His gaze had been on Chichester, but he looked at her now, and she thought she saw a shadow of something in those beautiful green eyes. "I am concerned it is our broken engagement that has kept Chichester from making a formal offer for your hand, and I wish to show him there is no ill will between us."

The words were spoken with a clear, calm voice, and

when he was finished, he looked away again as though he were simply commenting on the weather.

She reached up before remembering she wore a bonnet and could not, in fact, push her fingers through her hair. She let her hand drop and looked about them instead, at the clusters of people who dotted the lawn off Lady Satterwhite's terrace.

They were lucky the day had dawned bright and clear after the relentless rain of the previous day. Robert had collected Ingrid almost as soon as they arrived, and she saw them now next to a display of hothouse orchids. They were chatting with another couple and pointing out the orchids as if selecting their favorites. Her sister looked so carefree and happy, and Winnie pressed her hand more firmly to her stomach as if all of her rioting emotions pooled there.

"There is no ill will between us?" She could hardly form the words. She'd run away from Philip, leaving him stranded in the middle of a garden. He'd been forced to walk through a gauntlet of society's most noted and noteworthy alone, knowing news of their broken engagement would soon spread through the *ton*.

And that was only the physical components.

She had spent the past five years haunted by what she had done to him emotionally. She swallowed and forced her thoughts away before tears came to her eyes.

"Of course," he said, his voice just as calm and even. "I don't wish to stand in the way of your future happiness." He looked right at her as he said it, his voice like liquid fire, and she wanted so much to tell him he was her future, but that was a lie.

She looked away, swallowed, gathered herself, and—

"Greylock, isn't it?"

"Chichester," Philip said with enough enthusiasm she thought he might be greeting an old school chum. "I had hoped to make your acquaintance. I've heard interesting things about your land deals. Tell me. Might you have something in the works as we speak?" He gestured weakly to the group of men with whom Chichester had been speaking.

Winnie couldn't decide where to keep her eyes. What was Philip playing at? He had proclaimed Chichester a bastard of the first order. Everyone had heard it, including Chichester. But Chichester. Oh God, what was Philip thinking?

Heat crawled its way up her neck in anxious welts, and she tried to draw a restorative breath.

Everything hung on this single moment. Philip could stop it. He had the power to stop it all right then with just a single word, and Winnie had never felt more hopeless than she did in that moment.

But Philip didn't end it. Chichester did.

"I find that hard to believe considering what it is you said about me at the Waterloo dedication." Chichester might have been a scoundrel, but he was rather direct.

Winnie held her breath, unable to push her hands into her stomach any more without risking folding completely over.

"Ah, yes," Philip said, his expression never wavering. "That is precisely why I wished for this introduction. You see, there's been a misunderstanding." He smiled now and glanced briefly in Winnie's direction.

Oh heavens, she must breathe, or she would faint.

"I did call you a right many names, I'm afraid, Chichester, but that is because I heard you and Lady Winnaretta have an understanding."

This was it. Winnie was going to expire on the spot and crash directly into—she took a peek beside her at the topiary she had nearly knocked over—Dionysus. There were worse ways to go, she supposed.

"And I'm afraid I was rather heartbroken to hear of it. You

see, Lady Winnaretta is the finest woman I have ever had the pleasure of knowing, and I am quite devastated to hear she has chosen another. I had hopes that one day she would see me in a different light, but I am afraid that is not to be." His smile now turned dangerous. "She has clearly chosen the better man, and I am sorry I had such an unforgivable response to the news. Please do forgive me."

Had she already died? That could be the only possible explanation for what she just heard. Philip was proclaiming Chichester was the better man? It couldn't be.

Chichester's long face remained stoic, and Winnie worried that Philip's ploy wouldn't catch hold. But then—rather unexpectedly—Chichester let out a laugh, deep and ponderous, as he shook his head. He stepped forward and slapped Philip on the back, and suddenly Winnie saw the clever businessman the rest of the *ton* was used to with his overt, friendly gestures and warm voice. The same voice that only served to turn her stomach.

"Greylock, my good man. Have heart. I'm sure you'll find someone suitable one day." Chichester stepped to the side and stood close to Winnie. She braced herself, but he didn't so much as take her arm. "I'm sure I can safely say though she will never measure up to Lady Winnaretta."

Oh please. She clenched her teeth together in the semblance of a smile. She had to remember why she was here. "You flatter me, my lord." She forced herself to look directly into Chichester's cold dark eyes.

Could she truly survive a lifetime married to this man? She must. There was no other way.

Just then there was the sharp clink of silver against crystal, and Winnie realized Lady Satterwhite stood on the terrace steps, crystal goblet in one hand, knife in the other as she tried to gain everyone's attentions.

"Excuse me, dears. Excuse me. May I have everyone's attention?"

The space around them quieted into a hush as Lady Satterwhite held up the knife in her hand and smiled.

She wagged the knife somewhere behind Winnie as if she were gesturing to a good friend to be silent, but Winnie couldn't help but back up a bit, afraid the woman's grip on the knife would falter and the thing would come directly at her. But backing up meant her shoulder struck Philip's arms, and she jerked in surprise.

"What is it, darling?" This from Chichester on her other side.

She had instinctively looked up at Philip, catching his eye and seeing in it the heat with which she was so familiar. Her insides twisted again, and she wondered not for the first time what he was playing at. But she only turned an innocent smile in Chichester's direction. "It's nothing, my lord. Only my slipper finding a divot in the grass."

"Of course, darling. Allow me." He took Winnie's arm before she could protest, and she realized suddenly that Philip had accomplished the very thing she had set out to do. Chichester patted her arm and gave her that predatory smile he sometimes did as his cold eyes roamed over her possessively.

She smiled, remembering this was what she wanted. Mother would be pleased to hear that scandal had been averted, and this entire mess with Ingrid and Robert was nearly behind them.

"Ladies and gentlemen, it is my great pleasure to have you all in attendance today." Winnie had nearly forgotten Lady Satterwhite and turned her attention back to the woman in question. "My dear Harold and I have a lovely surprise for you today." Here she pointed with the knife again—really, someone ought to disarm the woman—and Winnie caught sight of Lord Satterwhite, smiling proudly at his wife from his perch behind the orchid display. "We have spent all spring working on a new variety of rose, and we are so happy to share it with you all today!" Here she let out a little squeak of happiness and waved the knife furiously in glee.

Winnie involuntarily reached out a hand to stop the woman from flailing the knife about at the same time as Philip. She eyed him as he eyed her, and they both snatched their hands back before anyone might see them.

"But!" Lady Satterwhite continued. "We thought we might have bit of fun as we announce our new rose variety to the world."

A bit of fun? Oh no.

"Yes, that's right, everyone," Lady Satterwhite went on as though hearing Winnie's thoughts. "The roses are located at the center of the maze—" Here she all but flung the knife over their heads, and Winnie couldn't help but duck, hoping the woman wouldn't lose her grip. She glanced over her shoulder to see nothing but a blank wall of yew hedge and turned back to their hostess. "You will all split up into pairs and make your way to the roses in the center of the maze. The first pairing to reach the center shall take home a cut of the new rose!" She all but cried this last bit as though she were offering someone a helping of the Crown Jewels.

Winnie remembered to smile before turning to Chichester. "How exciting," she said. "Shall we?"

"Wait!" Lady Satterwhite cried, calling over the sudden buzz of excitement as guests began to pair off. "What fun is it if you simply join your friend in conquering the maze?" She made a tsking sound as she shook her head. "Oh no. I shall choose the partners!"

Winnie's mouth fell open as a murmur of excitement passed through the gathered guests, marked with moments of outright cheer. Winnie was going to be sick. She eyed the topiary of Dionysus. Poor chap. He was really in for it today.

"The first pairing shall be Lady Ingrid Lowe and Lord Brandon, and Lady Katherine Sawyer with Mr. Robert Clarke!"

There was a tittering of glee at this announcement, and Winnie turned to see the couple Ingrid and Robert had been conversing with pair off as they swapped partners. Her sister was laughing as she took the taller man's arm and the other girl, Lady Katherine it must have been, was laughing as well at something Ingrid must have said.

Winnie couldn't help but smile then at seeing her sister so happy.

The smile soon vanished, however, and she was certain she'd never find it again because just then Lady Satterwhite cried, "And the next pairing shall be Lady Winnaretta Lowe and Lord Greylock!"

This time the announcement was not met with cheering. It was met with a gasp of shock and whispers of hardly controlled gossip. Lady Satterwhite looked right at Winnie then, and Winnie knew.

Lady Satterwhite had done this on purpose. She'd either been there that day on the viewing platform or more likely she'd read the gossip rags.

Winnie took a step forward, not realizing what she was about, but Philip caught her arm, spinning her about in the direction of the maze.

"Oh ho, see here, Chichester. I'm afraid your reputation proceeds you." Philip gestured behind them to Lady Satterwhite, his voice pitched for everyone to hear. "Clearly our hostess has chosen to separate you from the bright mind of Lady Winnaretta to make the odds more even for the other players." He leaned forward and slapped Chichester on the back. "We all know you're likely to win, mate. Do give us blokes a fighting chance."

This was met with an uproar from the other gentlemen present as they surged forward to clap Chichester on the back and sing their agreement with Philip's pronouncement.

Winnie had never seen the marquess look so glib.

"I say you're right, Greylock." He returned Philip's gesture with a hearty slap of his own to Philip's back. "Good luck in there!" he cried, much to the amusement of the men behind him, and propelled both Philip and Winnie into the maze.

*** * *

THEY HADN'T MADE it very far into the maze when Winnie stopped Philip with a hand on his arm.

"What was that about?" Her nostrils were tight, and he realized she was angry with him.

He hadn't counted on her being angry, and he also realized, of course, she would be. She had explicitly asked him to stay away from her. No, that was not what she'd said. She'd said they couldn't be seen together. That was something else entirely.

Still. He was going against her wishes, and he felt a sharp jab at the obvious anger he had caused. It didn't matter. He couldn't let her marry Chichester. Marriage was for the rest of one's life, and Chichester was a—

He pushed that thought down. He really must stop thinking the worst of people even if he disliked them.

"I believe I was apologizing for what happened earlier this week." He straightened and dropped his arms to his sides, appearing as nonconfrontational as possible.

Winnie's lips parted, and he could almost see the fire with which she wished to speak flaring in her eyes, but suddenly she snapped her lips shut, her eyes blinking. It was a beat before she said, "I suppose you were." The words were low, nearly mumbled.

Philip tilted his head. "And I also believe I was smoothing things over between you and Chichester. I am not so ignorant as to think my public pronouncement questioning the legality of his birth was taken lightly by a man like the marquess." More blinking. "I hope my apology was enough to clear up any confusion or assuage any hurt feelings my carelessness caused."

More blinking until finally she looked away, her hand going up in that familiar gesture he knew meant she was attempting to push her hair from her forehead, but again, she struck the rim of her bonnet. She dropped her hand and looked directly at him, her shoulders rolling back.

"Thank you," she said, surprising him. "I was concerned the events at the bridge dedication would upset things between the marquess and myself, and I thank you for being a gentleman about it." She looked about them as though suddenly realizing they were surrounded by towering hedgerows. "And as much as I would like to blame you for our current situation, I don't believe that's quite fair."

"I will accept blame. You know as much. My reckless behavior put you in this position, and for that, I am sorry."

Her eyes moved slowly back to him, and he hated the wariness he saw there. He tried to cast his mind back to five years ago, tried to remember the way of things between them. There had been a natural rapport, he was sure of it. Romantics would have called it a spark, an instant attraction, perhaps even love at first sight, but he didn't think of it that way. It was something deeper, wider, unfathomable. It was as though they had known one another all this time and had finally found each other again after a long, unavoidable separation.

But now he wondered if he had made that up, a conjuring

of his mind to grapple with the fact that he had planned to marry a woman he did not know.

She shook her head and made an aborted gesture toward her hair once more. "I suppose you shouldn't really apologize. If we wish to find blame in this situation, there are too many suspects to pick just one." She smiled then, a half smile of chagrin, and for a moment, he slipped back to five years ago, and instead of a hedgerow maze they were surrounded by wildflowers. "Suppose we ought to get on with this then?" She motioned toward the path they had unconsciously selected when they'd entered the maze.

He followed the line of her hand, and from somewhere came the shriek of laughter followed by a cascade of giggles and a laughing command to be silent or risk giving away their location. At least someone was enjoying this.

Philip offered Winnie his arm, and he didn't realize how much he wished for her to take it until the warmth of her hand seared through his coat sleeve.

They had gone several yards farther into the maze when a comfortable silence settled between them. The day was warm, the sun unfettered by a single cloud, but here between the hedges it was cool and comforting.

"I hope the events at the bridge dedication did not upset you." She looked at him quickly, and he smiled softly. "I mean the events celebrating the battle at Waterloo. I haven't forgotten that you lost someone dear to you in the war."

Her eyes widened in surprise, and she looked away quickly as if hurt. He laid a hand over hers against his arm and slowed them to a stop.

"I didn't mean to cause you further pain, my lady. It's only—"

She faced him so quickly he nearly backed into the hedgerow. "Winnie. For God's sake, it's Winnie. If you *my lady* me one more time, I shall create a new exit from this maze."

He didn't know whether to smile or apologize. He went with the latter. "I'm sorry, Winnie. I wish only for you to know William is not forgotten."

She stared at him, her lips slightly parted, and he didn't know at all what to say, so he said nothing until finally she whispered, "Thank you."

She took his arm then, propelling them onto the path once more.

This time she spoke first. "I take it your family is well."

He hated the inanity of the question, of how carefully they spoke to each other. There had been a time when they'd whispered feverishly in the dark of important, weighty things, their future unfolding before them with possibility instead of whatever it was that existed now, a kind of half reality where they were forever suspended, not at the beginning but neither truly at the end.

"Caroline is well. My parents are about the same," he said.

Winnie gave him a knowing look.

The animosity between his parents was nearly legendary, and her look was comforting. "And your father is adjusting to his title, I take it?" He knew mention of her father would alleviate the tediousness of the conservation. After all, he didn't know precisely how long this maze was, and he didn't particularly wish to spend the whole of it in uncomfortable silence with a woman he was once meant to wed.

"I think he has accepted his fate, but I do know he misses his work."

"Does the title not give him enough freedom to continue with his architectural projects?" He helped her over a root that had wandered into the pathway as they took another bend in the maze.

She shook her head almost immediately. "You know how

Father is. If he can't give his entire heart to a project, he won't attempt it."

Philip frowned, unable to stop the expression. "Tis a pity though, isn't it? That the world should lose such a brilliant mind as your father's?"

Her step faltered, and he looked down to see what might have caused her misstep, but she was looking at him, her eyes watchful, and it was his turn to lose his step. They stopped by some kind of unspoken agreement as he watched her watch him.

"You think my father brilliant?"

"You know I always have."

Her lips drew to a thin line before she said, "Not everyone thinks that."

He raised an eyebrow. "That's because people are uncomfortable with things with which they have no familiarity. Your father is free from such limitations, and I think it rather makes others jealous."

She crossed her arms and tilted her head as if he were some sort of display at an exhibit. "You really believe that."

"Of course I do," he said, crossing his arms to match her stance. "I have always done."

She seemed to absorb this, and he wondered just exactly what she was thinking. For the first time he wondered if Hawk were right in his direction. It was deuced difficult to pretend admiration for a scoundrel like Chichester, and he wondered just what exactly he had gotten himself into, but then Winnie shook her head and proceeded down the path once more.

She didn't take his arm this time, but instead, settled into a pace beside him that was loose and almost carefree, like the day he had found her amongst the wildflowers.

"William liked mazes."

The words startled him. She had never spoken of William

during their short engagement. Philip knew little of the man beyond the fact that he was a local squire's son. It was surprising to hear her speak of him so casually now. But she went on.

"He always dreamed of constructing a maze on his father's property one day." She reached out a hand, trailing it along the yew bushes as she had done that day to the wildflowers. "I wonder if he would have ever done it."

He wondered if this were the first time she had ever spoken of William, but he doubted he would have such an honor bestowed upon him.

"Was William like your father? Did he enjoy engineering endeavors?"

Winnie's smile came naturally, and he wondered of what she was thinking. "Oh yes, William was quite intelligent when it came to the construction of things."

"I wish I could have met him."

She looked at him again, that half-frightened expression on her face as though she couldn't quite believe he would speak of William. He wanted to ask her of it, but a peal of laughter cascaded through the hedgerows beside them, and a bush several feet in front of them trembled as though someone passed just on the other side of it.

They fell into silence again, but it was different this time, lighter and easier to carry. They reached another intersection, and by unspoken agreement they turned right.

"How is Lady Genevieve? I heard somewhere that she was married," he said after a time.

Winnie faltered in her step again, and he reached out a hand this time to catch her. He placed both hands on her shoulders as he helped her straighten, but he could see now his words had agitated her. She looked everywhere but at him, the temporary easiness suddenly shattered.

"I'm afraid I'm no longer in correspondence with Lady Genevieve."

The muscles at the back of his neck tightened. "You… aren't?" He wasn't sure how much to press, but he knew there was something not quite right here. Lady Genevieve Chippenham had been Winnie's closest and dearest friend five years previous. Winnie had even asked Lady Genevieve to be an attendant at the wedding. What could have happened to rupture such a strong friendship?

Winnie looked at the ground as she said, "Lady Genevieve and I are more of an acquaintance now than a friendship, I'm afraid." When she finally looked up, her brown eyes were melting and sad. "Things were…different…after." She strung the words together carefully as though tiptoeing around the thing that could not be said.

After she had lost the baby and ended their engagement.

Five years had passed since it had happened, and he thought society would have forgotten about it, but standing there, feeling Winnie stiffen under his hands as she spoke, he realized the thing he had missed.

While his life had gone on, Winnie's had not.

Society had forgotten about him almost immediately. It tended to do that for gentlemen. But it wasn't the same for women.

Winnie had lost a dear friend. Winnie had lost—

His eyes dropped to her stomach before he could stop himself, and suddenly the realness of her life swept around him like a cyclone. It was too much, too much pressing down on him. The guilt at not realizing what she carried with her while he had been free to move on with his life the moment she'd released him from the engagement. The sadness at the very real pain that still lingered in her gaze. At the longing that she so desperately tried to hide from him. The way she spoke so reverently about her deceased lover.

He could see her sadness too, in the trembling corners of her mouth as she tried to keep her expression neutral, in the way her eyes roamed over his face as if searching for something, something, something—

Something that would serve as an excuse. As forgiveness.

He kissed her at the same moment she kissed him.

Her arms came around him, her fingers clinging, her mouth devouring, and in that moment, he felt all of it.

Five years of separation. Five years of denial. Five years of starving for one another.

He shouldn't be kissing her. He knew that, but he couldn't stop. *Wouldn't* stop. The haunting look in her eyes prevented him from releasing her, and kissing stopped him from saying the words he knew would only drive her away.

She claimed to love the Marquess of Chichester. She claimed to wish to marry him, yet her kiss revealed her for the liar she was. But Hawk was right. She would keep up her charade if he pressed her because the person she needed to convince most of her lie was herself.

So he kissed her instead of telling her how he felt, pulled her into his arms, and held her tightly to his chest as though he would never let her go.

But he did let her go eventually, and after several seconds of awkward glances, aborted words, and the straightening of clothes, they continued walking and walking and walking, following the sounds of laughter that seemed so far away until they emerged into the center of the maze to see the Marquess of Chichester holding a potted rose, the clear victor of the afternoon's entertainment.

Philip stood carefully apart from Winnie as she congratulated the man she would marry.

CHAPTER 5

*S*he had forgotten about Genevieve.

Winnie sat in the theater box beside her sister, their parents behind them. Her mother said it was because it presented them best to society, but Winnie knew her mother didn't wish for everyone to see her father dozing in the second act.

Right then Winnie wasn't thinking about her father dozing. She wasn't even thinking about how terrible the actress was playing Bianca. Although Winnie wasn't so distracted as to miss how the woman was hiding pieces of her script throughout the props. She'd practically read every line from the first scene from inside a punch bowl.

But even that absurdity wasn't enough to pull her thoughts away from what Philip had done.

She cringed at the thought alone. It sounded as though Philip were guilty of something when it really wasn't that at all. It was only…it was only…

Philip was the only one to be able to do it.

He was the only one who could have opened her up like this, pried off the barrier that she had erected when she'd lost the baby, lost William. He was the only one able to do it because he'd been the only one there when it had all happened.

She wondered suddenly how he felt about William. His actions spoke of some kind of affection toward her, but she wondered how he felt about William. Yet he had asked about him anyway.

More than that, though, Philip was the only one who could possibly know what it meant to lose Genevieve.

Because that was it really. She'd lost her.

Genevieve had been a good friend, yes, but it was more about what she represented. Her friend had been a casualty, a side effect, a symptom of everything else. Winnie had lost William, the baby, and then Philip, and yet the world went on around her, the pieces of her life rearranging themselves until they formed a new truth. But that was just the problem. The pieces could rearrange themselves around her, but she remained the same.

She was still Winnie. Without William. Without the baby. Without Philip.

But everything else had gone, including Genevieve.

What else had she lost that she didn't know? Wasn't aware of? Hadn't realized yet?

It was as though her carefully laid plan had slipped in the past week. Nothing noticeable, of course, and certainly not enough to have her straying from her goal. It was just...

Philip had made her open her eyes again.

She'd been asleep. She knew that. It was safer, easier, to get on in a life that wasn't supposed to be hers, in a life that reflected none of the things she had anticipated. But Philip had broken her open for just a moment, and she'd gotten a glimpse of what had changed without her.

She'd carefully retreated again, but she feared what Philip had done was irrevocable. Absently she touched her lips and snatched her hand away as though her fingers were scorched.

The roar of applause shook her from her thoughts, and she realized the curtain had closed on the actors. She blinked and turned to find her sister clapping distractedly beside her even as her eyes scanned the boxes opposite. Winnie knew Robert was in attendance that night, and she wondered if he would visit their box.

"Well, I'm off then," her father grumbled from behind them as he pushed to his feet and mumbled his excuses to their mother.

Winnie couldn't make out his words, but she didn't need to. Her father had the same habit every time they went to the theater, and she was sure someone could set a calendar to her father's habits. In three minutes and fifteen seconds he could be found on the pavement outside the theater, his pipe between his lips, blowing smoke in billowing bursts into the streets.

Her father didn't care to smoke inside. He said it clouded his thoughts, but really, Winnie thought he just wanted to escape the idle chatter that marked the interlude.

She waited for her father to slip out before turning to her sister. "Do you remember Genevieve Chippenham?"

Ingrid wrinkled her nose as she turned to face her. "Genevieve? Of course I do. Why should you mention her?"

Winnie waved off her sister's question as though her inquiry were only of the vaguest concern. "It's just I heard her name the other day and wondered where she's been."

"Yorkshire, most likely," Ingrid said, her gaze returning to the opposite boxes. "She married that Elmont boy. The younger one." Her sister shook her head. "I hope it's a love match because that gentleman has nothing else to offer poor Genevieve."

"Ingrid." Winnie was surprised how sharply her sister's

name sprang to her lips, and for a moment she wondered if it was her mother who had spoken. But a quick look behind her showed her mother deep in the evening newspaper she had smuggled into the theater.

"Why so cross?" Ingrid feigned innocence. "She was your friend, and she abandoned *you* after all."

Her sister was right, but Winnie frowned anyway. "It isn't polite. Someone could hear."

Ingrid wrinkled her nose again. Winnie would need to speak to her sister later about making such faces. It just wasn't done, and it would be terrible should Lord and Lady Snowshill see her thusly.

"It's not as though it matters, Winnie. You know I've already chosen the man I shall marry. The rest of them don't matter." She swept her hand toward the theater as if this encompassed the entire population of marriageable gentlemen.

Winnie opened her mouth to point out the issue with her sister's statement, but the curtain to their box drew back and a footman announced the Marquess of Chichester. Winnie started as their mother dropped her newspaper on their father's vacated seat as if it had been there all along.

They weren't expecting the marquess that evening, and for a moment, Winnie feared she'd forgotten an engagement, but no. It couldn't be that. So what else was it? What had brought the marquess to their box that night? Was it to do with Philip?

A flash of cold passed over her, and she fiddled with the elbows of her gloves as an excuse to rub her arms where gooseflesh had appeared. Surely it wasn't to do with Philip. Everything had seemed to be smoothed over at Lady Satter-white's garden party.

The cold was instantly replaced with a flash of heat, and Winnie looked away as she tried to gather herself, but even as she prepared herself to receive the marquess her mind was filled with pieces of another man.

The touch of his lips. The familiarity of his kiss. The way he held her that felt so *right*.

She turned back, a smile firmly in place as Chichester entered the box. Pleasantries were exchanged, and the marquess was offered a seat before Robert arrived, and they were forced to do it all again. Somehow Winnie felt a modicum of relief at the sight of Robert though. Perhaps she wouldn't be forced to entertain the marquess alone.

"Chichester," Robert said as they resettled in their seats. "I haven't had a chance to say congratulations. The word at my club is that your endeavors at Sutton Cross are coming to fruition. You're to open the hotel this summer, is that right?"

Chichester smiled, and Winnie wondered if his lips had always been that thin. Did he always reek of pomade and stale sweat? What would it be like to see such a face every morning across the breakfast table for the rest of her life? She forced herself to divert her gaze to Robert, if only to stop the stampede of thoughts.

What had gotten into her?

The Marquess of Chichester was a perfectly acceptable gentleman. Yes, he was slightly older than she but by no more than twenty years. Yes, she had heard rumors that his business affairs were less than tidy, but she'd never heard whispers of anything more scandalous than that. He was surely not a first-rate bastard.

She coughed as Philip's words bubbled up in her mind, and she covered her mouth delicately to hide the blush that heated her face.

Chichester gave her a brief glance of concern before turning to the far more savory subject, that of his business prowess. "Yes, I thank you, young man. That is the very reason for my visit. It seems Sutton Cross is soon to be the premiere spa town on the east coast."

Ingrid tilted her head. "Did someone say that or are you surmising as much, my lord?"

Chichester laughed even as Winnie attempted to glare a hole through her little sister's head. "Ah, I see you have no mind for business, do you, Lady Ingrid?" He waved one hand carelessly in the air as if to dismiss it. "No matter. You are a woman after all, and I don't suspect you have the capability of understanding business."

This effectively ended Winnie's attempt to telepathically instill sense in her sister as she turned her attention to Chichester, those stampeding thoughts pushing dangerously close to the surface.

Something dark and heavy and rotting settled deep within her, and she pressed a hand to her stomach as if to stop it from making her sick. She let her eyes drift to her sister who had already diverted her attention to Robert, Chichester's comment either forgotten or never truly heard in the first place. Winnie must do this. She *must*.

Chichester's smile was smug—had she ever noticed him being smug before?—as he went on. "I've ensured Sutton Cross will be nothing if not a success. I have all but guaranteed it, my lady."

Ingrid wasn't listening, and Winnie nudged her sister with a small bump of her knee against hers.

Ingrid started, smiling instantly as she said, "Oh yes, yes, quite, of course," as if it were a proper response to simply string words together.

Luckily their mother saved them. "I have heard only the most wonderful things about Sutton Cross, my lord. I should love to see it one day." Her mother had a way of tilting her head just so, and even though she wasn't speaking to Winnie, Winnie nevertheless felt touched by her mother's support.

Chichester placed both hands on his knees. "Well, then you must see it. As soon as is possible. The hotel shall be opening in the next several weeks. You'll visit the first of August, I should think."

Shock registered in her mother's eyes but only for a second, and it wasn't as though Chichester saw it. He was already extending an invitation to Robert and his family. With the marquess's gaze diverted, her mother turned a pained look in Winnie's direction.

They had heard plenty about the marquess's development at Sutton Cross. The town had once been a small hamlet along the Norfolk coast, and her father had more than once pontificated on the positioning of the spa town. It was simply too close to the tidal marshes. Surely the water there was brackish at best. How on earth could such a place purport to be a spa town? Taking the waters there might make a person very ill.

But…well…they hadn't a choice really, did they? Winnie looked back in Chichester's direction just as Robert finished accepting the marquess's invitation to Sutton Cross. When the marquess turned to her, Winnie had her smile in place.

"That would be lovely, my lord." She forced the corners of her mouth to turn up even more. She risked a glance at her mother who sat slightly behind the marquess and didn't fail to notice her mother's look of abject horror. Winnie pressed on. "I think my father would love a chance to speak with you in more detail about your future wishes for the project."

Winnie feared her mother would fall directly out of her seat.

The marquess clapped his hands to his knees once more. "That's settled then. I'll make the arrangements just as soon as possible." He went to stand and took Winnie's hands in his as he did so, forcing her to gain her feet awkwardly between the resettled chairs. "I'm very pleased you've accepted my invitation, Lady Winnaretta." His breath was thick with the stink of salted fish, and she held her breath to keep from retching. "I know you will find your visit to Sutton Cross to be life changing." He gyrated his eyebrows at this, and she noticed the wayward, wiry gray hairs that stuck out from the flat darker strands.

"Life changing?" She heard herself ask, the only thing she could think of as she tried to divert her gaze from those stray hairs.

His smile was nearly feral. "Yes, Lady Winnaretta." He leaned closer, and Winnie feared she would lose what little control she still had over her stomach. "For both of us," he whispered in a rush of foul breath, and then with a final squeeze of her hand, he left.

* * *

THE ONLY RELIEF Philip had from the torment of Winnie's kiss was at dinner two days after the event in question. His grandmother held regular dinners at her home on Grosvenor Square in Mayfair for the family to gather and enjoy each other's company, as she claimed. Even though the woman had suffered a stroke in recent years, Philip knew the septua-genarian only saw it as a minor setback and employed the careful use of dinners to keep tabs on her burgeoning family.

Grandmother Regina had taken residence at Grosvenor Square after the death of her husband when Philip's own father had become the new marquess and taken over resi-dence at Hodge House, the family home in London. Not wishing to be underfoot, his grandmother had taken lease here in Grosvenor Square, and with the companionship of her youngest daughter, Philip's aunt Verity, had settled into a seemingly happy and comfortable existence.

Happy and comfortable were not the words Philip would

use to describe Hawkins Savage when Philip spotted him crumpled into a chair in the drawing room when he arrived for dinner.

"Hawk, are you ill?"

Hawk was always invited to a Hodge family dinner simply because Grandmother Regina adored him. Everyone adored Hawkins Savage. It was just something about his nature that made him exceedingly likable.

Hawk raised only his eyes from where he'd been studying the contents of the glass he held behind two fingers perched on the arm of his chair. Philip didn't miss the spark of alertness that erupted in his friend's eyes when he must have realized who was speaking to him.

He straightened immediately, setting the glass properly aside on the table beside him and pulling at his coat until he likely felt more presentable before standing to greet Philip.

"I'm perfectly fine. Thank you for your concern, old friend."

Did he choke on the last two words or was Philip imagining it?

"You don't look perfectly fine. Is there something on your mind?" He knew he was prodding an open sore, but he wouldn't stop. Philip knew with near certainty the cause of that sore was Caroline, and despite her ill-conceived crusade to save Philip from what she believed was Hawk's immoral influence, it was really Caroline who needed the protection now. It was something he had come to understand since his return to Hodge House several years ago, and the guilt of having left Caroline in the middle of his parents' animosity was still something that nagged him.

Of course he couldn't have known just how bad things had gotten, but he had seen the outcome in Caroline. He felt it in his gut, and he only hoped the end he imagined would come to be sooner rather than later. He didn't think Hawk could survive much longer.

Hawk blinked and looked about the drawing room as if looking for someone to save him, but it appeared they had been the first arrivals for dinner, and they were all alone in the drawing room.

"No, nothing in particular," Hawk said after a beat and raised his eyebrows. "How goes things on the Chichester front?"

Philip suppressed a grin at his friend's obvious deflection and said instead, "Caroline won't be joining us this evening. I'm afraid she said she isn't feeling well and stayed home."

Hawk's gaze skittered away but not before Philip caught the flash of alarm in the man's eyes. So that was how things were then. Philip hated the pulse of relief that went through him. If Hawk married Caroline, he would save her from the disaster that was his parents' existence in Hodge House, and then perhaps she would be safe. He hated thinking of Caroline in those terms, but he had a suspicion marrying Hawk may just make her happy.

"I'm…sorry to hear that," Hawk finally managed.

Philip decided to put the man out of his misery and said, "I kissed Winnie."

Hawk seemed to come to his senses faster than if Philip had tossed him headfirst into a water trough.

"You kissed her?" Hawk whispered as if they were in danger of being overheard. "When? Then or now?"

"This past Tuesday," Philip stated with perilous specification.

Hawk took a step back. "Philip, must I say such an action strays wildly from what I had suggested?"

They had made their way across the room to the sideboard that held an array of liquors and glasses, and Philip helped himself. Propriety dictated he wait for his host, but as his hostess that evening was his grandmother, he thought he might bend the rules.

He took his first sip before realizing Hawk must have done the same, and his eyes strayed to the abandoned glass Hawk had been holding when he'd walked in. He slid a glance to his friend and once more hoped the man knew what he was playing at.

"You mustn't," he said, answering Hawk's question. "It was not a calculated step on my part. It simply occurred."

"Kisses have a tendency of being unpredictable, I must admit, but perhaps you could have exercised a modicum of self-control."

Philip gestured with his glass. "That's precisely the issue, I'm afraid."

"What's the issue?"

They turned at the sound of a familiar voice in the doorway to find Dashiell Evers, the Earl of Amberley, striding toward them.

Hawk frowned. "Where's your lovely wife? Surely you haven't forced us to endure your company without the pleasure of hers?"

Dash's grin was almost smug. "Of course not. She's gone to find Aunt Verity and Grandmother Regina." Philip gestured to the glasses behind them, and Dash nodded in affirmation before saying, "So what's this about an issue?"

"Philip kissed Winnie," Hawk announced.

Dash's grin disappeared, his eyes widening in concern. "When? Before?"

"Tuesday," Hawk muttered.

Dash pinned Philip with a near scalding look as he accepted a glass from him. "That's terribly specific."

Philip looked to the ceiling as he considered it. "Tuesday a little past three o'clock in the afternoon," he clarified.

"Far too specific," Dash amended. "What's going on? I thought she wouldn't even see you."

"She won't," Philip said, and then thought better of it. "At least, she wouldn't before. We were rather…thrown together, I'm afraid. Lady Satterwhite's garden party."

Dash cringed. "You attended that? Even Audrey made our excuses, and we're still obligated to present ourselves as a newly married couple."

"She didn't put on one of those absurd games of hers, did she?" Hawk asked.

Philip nodded, and his friends drew in twin gasps of anguish.

"Let's hear it then," Hawk finally said when he'd recovered enough to speak.

Philip spent the next several minutes explaining what had happened in Lady Satterwhite's maze with the exception of the topic of conversation at the moment of the kiss. That he kept to himself because it still brought him pain.

After losing so much, Winnie had lost her best friend on top of it.

In his mind, Winnie had been frozen in a moment in time. Her face in the moonlight as she peered up at him and broke his heart. It had never occurred to him that time had moved on for her just as it had for him. Only time had not been as fair to her.

Dash crossed his arms over his chest, his head tilting farther and farther as Philip's explanation progressed. Finally, he said, "So you're not sure if you kissed her or if she kissed you?"

"I think they kissed each other," Hawk added.

Philip looked between his two best friends. "Does it matter who did the kissing? The fact is it happened. It proves I was right. She's not in love with Chichester."

Dash dropped his arms, his eyebrows going up. "Chichester? Are you talking about the Marquess of Chichester?"

Hawk filled him in on Philip's belief concerning Winnie's assertion about her impending engagement.

"I agree with you," Dash said with a firm nod. "Chichester is a bastard of the first order. Have you ever seen the man play whist?"

"Whist?" Hawk repeated with a concerned twist to his lips.

Dash nodded again. "The man takes far too much pleasure in besting ladies at the game. His favorite prey are the old ones."

Philip frowned. "I'm not surprised."

They were interrupted by the arrival of Audrey, along with Aunt Verity and Grandmother Regina, and the conversation turned to greetings and catching up. Soon Philip's parents arrived, along with Aunt Eugenia, and the conversation spilled over once more. Philip's cousins Ethan and Gavin were the last to arrive, and they immediately pulled Philip, Hawk, and Dash aside, likely in an attempt to avoid Aunt Eugenia, their mother.

It was nearly time for dinner when Aunt Verity touched his arm. He turned, a smile already coming to his lips. Aunt Verity was closer in age to himself than to his parents, and he'd always gotten on with her rather well because of it. He couldn't help but notice she looked tired that evening, and he wondered if caring for Grandmother Regina after the woman had suffered a stroke was beginning to wear on her.

Her smile, though, was warm as she said, "Grandmother would like to speak to you if you have a moment."

He nodded and followed his aunt across the room to where his grandmother had settled her Bath chair by the fire. Her face opened as he approached, her lips curving into a genuine smile.

"Philip, is that my little boy?"

He bent to press a kiss to her cheek and inhaled her familiar lilac scent. "It is, Grandmother. Although I like to think I'm not quite so little anymore."

She pulled his hand into her own and patted it gently. "You will always be a wee lad to me, Grandson. Now then, where is that enchanting wife of yours?"

Philip glanced up at Aunt Verity who perched behind Grandmother's Bath chair, but she only firmed her lips and gave a slight shake of her head.

"I'm afraid I haven't a wife, Grandmother," he said gently, squeezing her hand reassuringly.

Grandmother waved him off. "Oh, I had forgotten. You didn't marry her, did you, Philip? Rather careless of you, wasn't it?"

He couldn't help but smile at this. "Yes, Grandmother, I'm afraid you're right."

She patted his hand. "I'll allow you to make it up to me though."

"You shall?" He smiled harder, but he couldn't help but feel a shadow cast over his happiness. Grandmother Regina was getting on in years, and he knew conversations such as this were numbered. He pushed the thought away, determined to enjoy the conversations they did have left.

"Yes. I shall allow you to accompany me to Bath."

He stilled, his smile faltering. "I'm sorry?"

Grandmother Regina was nodding. "I find the hustle of London is getting frighteningly too much for me, my grandson, and I should like to be away. To Bath, I should think. They say the waters are restorative."

Philip glanced up at Aunt Verity, but the woman wasn't looking at them, her gaze drifting somewhere across the room. It might have been the odd angle or the firelight reflecting, but he thought Aunt Verity appeared almost wistful just then.

He looked away when Grandmother Regina squeezed his hands again. "Young man, did you hear me?"

He forced a smile now. "Yes, I did hear you, Grandmother. It's only I have commitments here in London, and I shouldn't wish—"

She let go of his hand now to raise both of her own. "Oh, it's nothing like that, boy. I know we are in the midst of the season. I shouldn't like to pull you away just now." She leaned forward, her Bath chair squeaking softly. "Tell me, young man. Is there another young thing that has caught your eye?"

Philip's smile came more easily once again. "Grandmother Regina," he scolded playfully. "To speak of such things in mixed company."

Grandmother Regina laughed, the sound bringing the attention of Audrey and Hawk who had gathered on the opposite side of the fireplace.

"What is quite so funny, Grandmother?" Audrey asked.

Grandmother Regina waved a hand at Philip as he stood, allowing his cousin and friend to approach the older woman.

"Philip, my boy. Has he always been such a prude?"

Philip nearly choked on the sip of his drink he'd just taken, and Hawk slapped him heartily on the back. Rather too heartily, and Philip sent him a glare, but Hawk only laughed.

"I'm afraid you've got it in one, Grandmother Regina. You know my boy, Philip here. He would never do anything to upset a lady." Hawk's gaze was far too piercing for casual conversation, and Philip couldn't help but meet his friend's eyes.

Because Hawk was right. He wouldn't do anything to upset a lady. At least, he thought he wouldn't. But that was before Winnie had kissed him, confusing the issue entirely.

CHAPTER 6

"Where is he?" Winnie did all she could to survey the ballroom without being so obvious as to stand on her toes.

"He said he would be here," her mother whispered from beside her.

Winnie glanced in her mother's direction, envying the woman her height in that moment. Her mother was not at risk of resorting to standing on her toes to see the attendants at Lady Nottaway's ball.

"Are you sure he said Lady Nottaway?" Winnie whispered in return.

Her mother nodded and finally turned in Winnie's direction. "He promised he would be here before the dancing started."

At this they both slid a glance in Ingrid's direction, and Winnie's heart twinged. Her sister looked so pretty standing there in the candlelight, her ivory gown sprigged with tiny rosebuds that drew out her warm color. Her golden hair twisted into curls that framed her face. She looked like a fairy from a Norse myth.

And yet her dance card remained empty.

Ingrid attempted a smile when she caught them peering at her. "It's not as though I haven't tried," she all but hissed. The thing that Ingrid had tried was to learn how to properly dance. No matter how many dance tutors Winnie's mother hired or how many tricks Winnie herself tried to teach her sister to remember the steps, her success in dancing matched that of her success in embroidery. And watercolors. And the pianoforte. "You know the steps just get all tangled in my head."

Winnie tried very hard not to frown. It was true. Her sister had tried, and still she could not muster a simple waltz let alone the intricate steps of a quadrille. This left Ingrid in an unfavorable light should Lord and Lady Snowshill see her relegated to the periphery of the ballroom.

"I know, darling." Their mother squeezed Ingrid's arm reassuringly. "Cousin Frederick said he would be here to start the dancing with you. I am sure he hasn't forgotten."

Her mother slid Winnie a look then that suggested she thought otherwise. That perhaps Frederick hadn't forgotten and was simply trying to avoid having his toes mangled by Ingrid's messy attempts at a cotillion.

Winnie bit her lip and went back to surveying the ballroom. Surely her cousin would show up soon. Winnie had been so careful to choose only invitations that would position Ingrid to her advantage. Namely ones where a trusted family member would be present to ask Ingrid to dance. It would not do at all to have her sister sitting with the wallflowers and spinsters tonight. She must do something. But what? It wasn't as though *she* could ask her sister to dance.

"He's not in the card room, I'm afraid." Her father approached them, his unlit cigar in one hand, a glass of punch in the other.

"Thank you for checking, Carl." Mother squeezed his arm

much as she'd done with Ingrid. "I suppose we'll…" But her voice trailed away without concluding the sentence.

Winnie's chest tightened, and she frantically searched the room. There must be someone in attendance who would help her. But as soon as the thought entered her mind, she remembered her conversation with Philip. Her circle of friends had shrunk, catastrophically, in the past five years, and when her father had unexpectedly inherited the title, it had shifted the family into an awkward half existence. Their friends from before no longer called as regularly or stopped to talk about the use of lintels in Greek architecture with Father. And yet, as unexpected heirs, they didn't quite fit in with the rest of the *ton* to which they now seemingly belonged.

This would never do. She gathered her skirts, prepared to circle the room to find anyone—even Chichester if she must —but she would find—

"Lord Bibury, what a pleasant surprise."

Philip.

Winnie spun about far too quickly, and because she held her skirts in her hands, she made a terrible swishing noise that drew glances from the guests nearest them. The glances turned into stares when the same guests realized what was happening about them.

Not Philip. Anyone but Philip. He may have smoothed things over with Chichester, but she had meant what she'd said that day at the bridge dedication. They couldn't be seen together. Too much hung in the balance, and one wrong whisper could upset everything.

Philip made a small bow to Winnie's father. "I'm very sorry about the death of your brother, my lord. Such a tragic loss. I am sure you grieve still."

Winnie's father gestured with the unlit cigar. "Greylock! I say. Didn't expect to see you. How are you, my good man?"

Father never called Chichester by such an amiable term. It truly didn't matter what her father called Chichester, and yet it still irked.

There were several exchanges of pleasantries then while each man asked after the other's family before Philip said, "I was hoping to find you this evening actually. Did you see the evening *Times?*"

Father gave Mother a knowing look then, and Winnie suspected Mother had absconded with the evening edition of the newspaper before Father had a chance to see it.

"I'm afraid I haven't had the pleasure as of yet."

"They're saying some Italian chap has formed an expedition to go into Egypt to uncover antiquities there."

Father's cigar stilled. "Egypt? That can't be."

Philip nodded. "Apparently this Belzoni man went into Egypt to showcase a hydraulic machine of all things. The Egyptian government is apparently pushing for some agrarian advancements. The entire thing has turned into an antiquities endeavor."

Father pointed with his cigar. "I say, I hope the man knows what he's doing. There are examples of Egyptian architecture that continue to boggle the modern mind. I shouldn't wish for them to be the victims of carelessness and greed."

Philip nodded. "That's precisely why I had hoped to find you. You've had some experience with this in Greece, haven't you?"

Winnie stilled, a sense of knowing flowing over her body like a silk gown.

Philip knew precisely what he was doing. He knew the one thing her father could not avoid speaking of was his time in Greece. And then the blasted man slid his gaze ever so imperceptibly to her and then—he wouldn't, and yet he did! —he had the nerve to tip up just one corner of his mouth.

She looked away, heat springing up her neck. What was he doing? What game was he playing? Did he think—oh God, did he think she had changed her mind? Did he think that kiss in the maze meant something? That she was giving him permission to pursue her?

The thought sent euphoria spiraling through her. God, if she could only marry Philip—

She gave herself a mental shake. Philip was precisely the reason she must do what she had intended. She turned away and went back to scanning the crowd. Ingrid must secure a partner for the first dance. Anything less simply wouldn't do.

She was jolted from her perusal within seconds when the first notes of a violin crept over the dull buzz of conversation. Her gaze flew to the dais at the far end of the room, and the sight of a single violinist sent terror through her.

The orchestra was starting to arrive.

Once more she plucked at her skirts to begin her search in earnest when a hand at her elbow stopped her. She jumped and pressed a hand to her chest and then immediately backed away when she realized it was Philip who had touched her elbow. She slid her gaze behind him to find her father had been absconded by a professor from the university where he had once taught. Her mother was unhelpfully distracted by repairing a loose hairpin in Ingrid's coiffure.

Philip leaned close. "You seem upset, Winnie. Can I help?"

"Don't call me Winnie in public," she hissed and immediately hated herself.

Philip took the smallest of steps back, and her heart sank. But more, her stomach churned at the realization of what she had done, of what she had become, snapping at him like this.

"I'm sorry, Philip," she said, more softly this time. She raised a hand, and she realized she had thought to touch him, and she snatched her back, her eyes unable to keep away from his.

There had been a time when she could have touched him like that. Without thinking. Just because she wished to. But that time had passed.

"I'm truly sorry," she said again, but this time she held his gaze.

He stepped closer to her. "You seem to be distressed. Please tell me how I can help."

And wasn't that the worst thing about Philip Hodge. He always wanted to help her.

But he couldn't help her, not with this and not now. He couldn't stop her from marrying Chichester because he was the very reason for her fall from grace. And now she must pay for it.

She shook her head, controlled and carefully so as not to raise further suspicion. "It's nothing. I assure you. It's only our cousin promised my sister the first dance this evening, and he's not here."

Philip's brow furrowed. "Why is her intended not partnering her?"

"Because his parents—" It was all she could do to stop the runaway words and keep her terrible secret from tumbling from her lips. She straightened and drew a much-needed, steadying breath. "Because his parents have been delayed, and they have not yet arrived," she said instead of admitting the truth of it. That Robert's parents were wary of their son's relationship with Ingrid and partnering her for a dance had been tabooed.

Philip raised an eyebrow at this, and she hoped fervently that her lie was true. She hadn't spotted Robert yet, but that didn't mean he wasn't present. The room was filled to bursting. Anyone could be in attendance, including dear Frederick, and not be seen for a good hour or more. She had to only hope that Philip wouldn't see the Clarkes and find her out.

She studied his face, but his eyebrow never calmed. Nor

did he speak. Or blink. He kept his quiet, curious gaze trained on her face, and she felt with each second the need to say something. But if she spoke now, she very much feared she'd blurt out every terrible thing.

Suddenly they were no longer standing in the Nottaway ballroom. They were somewhere else and some *when* else again. And Philip had come to save her then too, and she suddenly wanted to lay her head on his chest and let him take away her burdens.

But she couldn't. God, she couldn't. She must be stronger than this. Tears smarted at the backs of her eyes, and she was forced to turn away. Was love meant to hurt this much? Her gaze fell on her sister, smiling now as the rest of the orchestra took their seats, and the hum of the violin was joined with the thrumming of a cello and the whistle of a piccolo.

Smiling and expectant and…hopeful.

Winnie swung about. "Dance with my sister." The words sprang from her lips at the same time she grabbed Philip's arm. "Please. I need you to dance with my sister."

Later she would think about all the ramifications. She would think and worry and ruminate about what this would mean should Chichester hear about it. What other members of the *ton* would say, of the rumors that were likely to flare up because of what was about to happen.

But she couldn't think of that right now. Right now she had to present her sister in the best light to the rest of society, and the best light unfortunately had Philip Hodge standing it.

Philip's smile was quick, somehow knowing, and she knew there would be questions later. But later was still later, and right now her sister must dance.

* * *

LADY INGRID LOWE could not dance.

At first he thought the events of the past few weeks had addled his brains, but by the fourth turn about the floor, he realized it was not he who was making missteps, but rather Lady Ingrid. She smiled soundly enough and dazzled the fellow dancers with her exuberance, but her steps, well, they left much to be desired. He'd even been forced to save her from spinning into the refreshment table.

A sheen of sweat had broken out over the whole of his body by the time he returned her to her family, Winnie's absence from the small group most notable.

"Thank you, Lord Greylock." Ingrid still beamed, her cheeks rosy with the effort of dancing, serving only to make her appear more delectable, like a cherry confection on a tea tray. "That was most exhilarating."

Was the girl oblivious to her shortcomings or simply chose to ignore them? Either way he found her happiness at the conclusion of what was to him the worst dance he'd been forced to endure rather charming.

He bowed and had just bid farewell when he caught the tell-tale flash of lavender disappearing behind the row of seated matrons on the other side of the refreshment table. Trying not to look as though he were in pursuit, he skirted his way through the refreshments, dodging a pair of sisters he had the unfortunate fate of having been introduced to once only to discover they only spoke when one could complete the other's sentences, and found himself in the corridor to the retiring rooms.

Another flash of lavender and he turned, catching the last glimpse of Winnie as she made her way about the corner at the far end of the corridor. He nodded at the few guests who lingered on their way back to the ballroom, and as casually as possible—and without outwardly wincing, even though his toes begged him to stop and put up his feet—he made his way to the end of the corridor just as Winnie opened the door to the first retiring room on the left.

He caught it before she had a chance to shut it behind her and lock him out, and none too delicately shoving her inside, he snapped the door shut behind him and sent the bolt home before turning on her.

"Your sister can't dance."

Her eyes were wide, and her lips were parted. "This is a retiring room, Philip," she whispered, although there was no chance they would be overheard.

"I'm aware. It just so happens I'm in need of some retirement." He dropped to the settee pushed into the corner of the small room and lifted one foot, prying the boot off, much to the relief of his crushed toes. He eyed Winnie as he massaged the offended appendages.

"It's a *ladies* retiring room, Philip."

"I thought we weren't to use given names."

Her lips pursed in obvious disapproval, but instead of arguing further, she perched on the edge of the chair opposite, her hands falling to her lap.

"You know your sister cannot dance," he went on. It wasn't a question, and at least she had the decency not to deny it.

"It's not that she hasn't tried," she said in immediate defense.

Philip switched feet, once more prying loose his boot to cast it aside. Winnie watched his boot sail across the room, but she wisely did not say anything.

"And you must now conscript family members into service as her dancing partner?"

"Something like that," she muttered and looked away.

He dropped his foot and leaned forward, bracing his elbows on his knees. "Winnie, I believe you owe me an explanation."

She leaned forward too, bringing her face close enough to his so he could see the gold striations in her irises. "I owe you nothing."

"My toes say differently."

She looked down at his stockinged feet at this and wrinkled her nose. "It couldn't have been that terrible."

"It was only through careful placement of my poor feet that I prevented your sister from knocking Lady Fullerton's wig from her head."

Winnie sat back finally, her shoulders rounding, her expression far more understanding as it should have been. "Then I suppose I should apologize for not warning you."

He took advantage of her averted gaze and grasped her hand. With a single tug, she spilled toward him and the settee, and he neatly caught her against him. He cupped her face in one palm and forced her to look at him.

"Winnie, I know something isn't right. I've known since that first day I saw you again at the bridge dedication. You must tell me what's wrong so I can help." He studied her eyes, her bottomless brown eyes, and in them he saw so much.

It had always been that way. Looking into Winnie's eyes was like unraveling a fairy tale that painted magic and wonder page after page. Right then, though, he saw pain in them, pain and worry and...fear.

He pulled her more snuggly against him. "Please, Winnie. Tell me."

"Robert's parents do not approve of the match." She spoke so softly he nearly missed it.

His arms loosened about her in confusion. "Robert's parents?"

Winnie nodded, her cheek rubbing against his palm. "Lord and Lady Snowshill did not give Robert their blessing to ask for Ingrid's hand."

He dropped his own hand then but kept a single arm

about Winnie's shoulders as if by touching her he could believe what she said was real. He had imagined any number of reasons why she would be acting so oddly, why she would run from him and demand they not be seen together in society, that they use their titles even after all they had been through, but not this.

"Lord and Lady Snowshill?"

She nodded, her hair crackling against his arm, and he released her fully then, but he didn't move away from her on the settee and neither did she, their bodies staying pressed together as though taking unconscious comfort from one another.

"Robert will one day be the Viscount Snowshill. It's an old title, and with such prestige comes a great deal of concern for its future. Lord and Lady Snowshill are reserved about the match."

"And this…" He gestured weakly around them as if to encompass the whole of their interactions.

"We're trying to present Ingrid in the best light to help Lord and Lady Snowshill see that she is a good match for Robert."

He looked sharply at her. "That's why you've suddenly reentered society?"

She sat up at this. "Reentered?" She gave a weak laugh. "Philip, I never left it."

"Yes, you did." It was his turn to give her a quizzical look. "Winnie, you haven't been to a single social function before this season. Not for the past five years."

Her eyes focused on him suddenly. "You've been keeping track."

He frowned. "All of society has been keeping track. I'm afraid to say there have even been wagers placed on when you would return. It's in all the betting books at the clubs."

Her lips parted, her eyes rounding in confusion. "But I

never went anywhere." She spread her arms. "I've been here the whole time."

"No, you haven't." He didn't know why he whispered the words, but a concern had taken hold of him, much deeper and sadder than any he had felt before for Winnaretta Lowe.

"I—" She licked her lips and looked around at the retiring room, but her shoulders slumped as though the argument had left her.

He slipped his hand into hers and pulled it to his thigh where he could hold it against him as though to anchor her to him. "Winnie, I'm sorry I wasn't there." He felt the words on his tongue, but it was as though they were covered in barbs, and no matter how he spoke them, he knew it would hurt him all over again. "I'm sorry I wasn't there when you lost the baby."

Her hand tugged against his as he knew it would, as her natural instinct to flee from the thing that gave her pain was triggered at his words, but he held her fast against him until she stilled. When she looked at him, her eyes were damp, her lips parted, but her chin remained firm.

"You mustn't apologize. It wasn't…it wasn't…" She didn't finish the sentence but instead looked away.

"You're right. I mustn't. But I still feel what I feel, and I want you to know that." This drew her gaze back to him, but this time a single tear had fallen, leaving a trail down her cheek. He wanted to reach up, stroke her cheek, pull her back against him, but he held himself still.

This wasn't about that. Not now. There were words inside of him that had been waiting five years to come out, and he would say them now. "When I realized what had happened, that night in the garden when you told me I was released from the engagement, I knew what you hadn't said, and I was…sad." He gave a brittle laugh then and felt his own tears prick his eyes. "It's such a small word, sad, but it's how I felt. This complete and thorough sadness that I thought might drown me because I was no longer going to get to meet this tiny person you were carrying."

"Julia."

He had been studying the carpet, watching his toes curl into the fibers and back up in order to keep the tears from falling, but he looked up at this, at her. "Julia?"

She nodded, and he realized her eyes had cleared. "I named her Julia."

He shifted on the settee to better look at her. "You thought her a girl?" He shook his head, laughing weakly once more. "I always felt he was a boy."

"What?" The single word was thick with confusion, and he squeezed her hand.

"I know it sounds silly, but I—" He shook his head as if to shake away the cobwebs of his own thoughts. "I just had this feeling that he was a boy." He smiled now at the memory, and he said things he hadn't meant to say. "I could picture what it was going to be like when I took him to pick out his first pony just as my father had done with me."

"Oh Philip." The tears were in her voice then, and she pulled his hand toward her now, wrapping her other hand about it and holding it as though to comfort him, which was not what he'd intended, but somehow he couldn't bring himself to break the moment. "I never knew you felt that way."

She had never given him the chance to tell her. She broke their engagement and begged him to leave her be before she'd run away into the night. But he didn't say that. Instead he said, "I never got the chance to tell you." Words that cast the blame on him even when he didn't deserve it.

"I'm sorry, Philip." Her voice was stronger now, but he didn't know what she was sorry for any longer, and he only wished to see her smile again.

He cupped her face with his free hand. "It's all right, Winnie." He spoke the words as sincerely as possible. "My toes shall recover."

She laughed then, the sound more of a snort as it caught her by surprise. She pressed a hand to her lips as if to stop the faux pas, but this only made her laugh harder, and then noise struck her fingers, distorting it even further.

He let go of her hand to stand and waddled exaggeratedly across the small room in the direction of his discarded boot. Her laughter grew the more he waddled, and he stopped at the vanity pressed into the opposite corner, plucking a strawberry from a tray that had been left on it.

He turned to her. "You get refreshments in your retiring rooms? I'm never using the gentlemen's again." He popped the strawberry into his mouth as she dissolved into laughter.

"Philip, you must stop. Someone shall hear." She looked to the door as if they were in danger of getting caught.

He found one boot and then the other and waddled back to the chair she had perched on earlier. "I meant what I said, Winnie. I should like to help with your sister's predicament."

He watched her face carefully for though she said her sister was trying to secure an engagement her intended's family did not approve of, Winnie had said nothing about her own impending engagement. This only served to pique his interest further, and now more than ever, he felt driven to find out why she would pursue such a less than acceptable gentleman.

But Winnie shook her head as she stood and shook out her skirts, going to the mirror over the vanity to check her coiffure. "It needn't matter, Philip, but I appreciate the offer."

"Why doesn't it matter?" he asked, shoving one foot into the waiting boot before picking up his other foot to do the same.

She turned from the mirror. "We're leaving London week after next."

He stilled, his second boot forgotten in his hands. "Leaving London?"

She nodded. "We've been invited to Sutton Cross."

He dropped the boot and the foot that remained unshod to stand and limp the few steps across the carpet to where Winnie stood.

"Sutton Cross? Chichester's supposed new spa town?"

Her frown caused a wrinkle to appear between her brows. "Not supposed. It's finished. The hotel is opening the beginning of August. Father's quite excited about it. He's never stayed in a hotel with over one hundred rooms."

"Is that so?"

She nodded and plucked a strawberry for herself from the tray on the vanity. "Yes." She studied him thoughtfully as she chewed. "Why?"

Philip shook his head. "It's nothing. Just idle curiosity." He went back to the chair to finish with his boot, but his thoughts were already churning. "I suppose you're going to take the waters there."

There was a moment's hesitation, and he looked up to find her biting her lower lip. "Yes, I suppose we shall," she muttered finally.

He stood and felt a sharp pain travel over his toes at the movement. He tried to hide the wince as he said, "I've heard taking the waters does wonders. My grandmother swears by it." He smiled despite the pain.

Winnie might be leaving London, but then, so was he apparently.

CHAPTER 7

He thought the baby was a boy.

It wasn't until much later in the small hours of the morning when she was back home, sitting at her dressing table brushing out her hair, Mathilda in the background putting away Winnie's things, that Winnie let the thoughts come into her mind and wander for a bit.

Until that moment in the ladies' retiring room, Julia had been her secret alone. She had never told anyone about naming the baby Julia, but when Philip had whispered those words, speaking of the future they had anticipated but never gotten, it wasn't until that moment she realized she hadn't been alone five years ago.

A different pain burned low in her stomach now as she thought of it.

Five years ago she had been so ashamed of falling in love with Philip when her lover whose baby she carried was lost somewhere on the Continent, his body never to be recovered, that she hadn't thought when she found herself no longer in need of a husband. She'd simply run away from the cause of her shame.

No, that wasn't right.

Philip didn't cause her shame. It was her. Herself. Her weak character.

She studied her reflection in the mirror as if she could see the weakness written across her features. But it was just the same face she'd always seen, the slash of dark eyebrows, the full mouth, and rounded cheeks, the whisper of freckles. It was all just her, but there was so much more than that. So much she was only now learning she'd never overcome.

She gripped the edge of her dressing table, resolve hardening inside of her.

She must marry the Marquess of Chichester. It was the only right thing she could do now.

The sound of her dressing room door closing behind her tugged her from her thoughts, and she turned slightly to see Mathilda laying her dressing gown across the foot of the bed, straightening the quilts as if she hadn't already done it several times already.

"Mathilda."

The maid straightened, her lips firm, her eyes direct. "Yes, my lady?"

Winnie pivoted on her stool as she tried to form the question she wished to ask. "Do you remember when…" Oh God, how to ask this question? "Do you remember the trouble I had a few years ago?"

Mathilda crossed her hands in front of her. "The baby, my lady?"

Winnie sucked in her lower lip. Mathilda was never one to skirt the issue at hand. "Yes, the baby. Do you…" What was the question she was even attempting to ask? "Do you recall that period well?"

Mathilda nodded once. "Yes, my lady. I always remember. My lady was very sad during that period."

Winnie nodded and stood, pressing her palms into the

tops of her thighs as she did so as if gaining strength from her own body. "Yes, it was a very sad time." She took a step toward the bed but was startled to find Mathilda had moved, coming suddenly around the bed to stand only a couple of steps in front of Winnie.

"No, I did not say it was a sad time. I said it was you who was sad, my lady." Mathilda always had a way of bending her head to get within Winnie's line of sight as the woman's towering stature dwarfed Winnie's diminutive one. "You are always doing this, my lady. Always. Since you were little." Here the woman gave a small shake of her head, her hair never shifting from the tight braids she always wore wrapped about her head.

"Doing what?" Winnie made to retrieve her dressing gown from the bed, suddenly feeling exposed in only her nightrail.

"You make yourself a nest."

Winnie turned back to the maid at this. "I make myself a…nest?"

Mathilda nodded once with exacting affirmation. "Yes, a nest. You're like a bird. You construct a nest you want no others to see, but if they get too close, you fly away. As if they will not learn the truth from a distance. As if they cannot see that far." Here she stuck out a single finger to point in Winnie's direction. "But sadness such as the kind you bore can be seen from great distances. No matter how you try to stay away."

The maid turned before Winnie could say anything and began to gather Winnie's discarded stockings and slippers.

Winnie took a step toward her but stopped, lost in her loyal maid's words at the same time she feared them.

"Mathilda, do you remember Genevieve?" Winnie said before she could think better of it. "Genevieve Chippenham?"

Mathilda didn't stop her straightening of the room. "Yes, Miss Chippenham is a very good friend to you."

Winnie almost caught herself on a bark of laughter at the thought. "I'm afraid she was a very good friend. But maybe not so good as I haven't seen her in several years. Not since…" She fingered the quilt Mathilda had folded back on her bed as if to distract herself with the fine embroidery. It was several seconds before Winnie realized the rustling in the room had stopped. She looked up to find Mathilda holding her chemise in one hand, stockings in the other, her expression a mixture of confusion and concern.

"Miss Chippenham is a very good friend, my lady. She tried so very hard to see you when you were taken ill."

Winnie shook her head. "You must be confused, Mathilda. Miss Chippenham didn't call on me."

Mathilda's expression grew more concerned. "Of course she did, my lady. A great many of your acquaintances from that time tried to call on you, but you asked me to keep them at bay."

"That's not—" She stopped, the words clogging her throat as she thought of that day Philip had tried to call on her, and her instinctual reaction was to send Mathilda to deal with him. She swallowed as if she could swallow down the words she had meant to say, but she was left speechless instead.

Mathilda took a single step forward. "You asked me to keep them all at bay, my lady. You said you wished to be alone. That they couldn't know of what you'd done." The maid shook her head. "It always confused me as I think everyone knew of the baby. A hasty engagement and a hastier wedding to plan." More head shaking. "Everyone must know surely, and yet you held yourself so carefully away from it all as if you didn't wish to share your heartbreak with anyone else. So much like the bird who flies away from the very first suggestion of danger."

When Mathilda spoke like that, it sounded all so terribly selfish, but that wasn't how Winnie remembered it. In fact, all Winnie could remember was the darkness and the pain.

She sat down on the edge of the bed, her hand straying to the carved post at one corner as if to hold herself upright as the memories came flooding back to her. The moment she realized something was wrong, the physical pain that lanced through, and then—

The blood. So terribly much. It was everywhere, and she couldn't stop it. She had reached down there, scrambling to get her skirts out of the way as if she could hold the baby inside of her, would hold the baby inside of her for the next seven months if it meant Julia would stay alive.

But she hadn't. She hadn't kept the baby alive.

There was blood, and then there was darkness.

The bed dipped as Mathilda sat beside her and took Winnie's free hand into her own.

"Do you know how long I was lying there before you found me?" Winnie finally whispered.

Mathilda shook her head quietly now. "Too long. You were very sick for many days."

Winnie remembered trying to find a chamber pot when the bleeding started, crawling across the floor as she feared standing would cause the baby to slip out, but she didn't remember anything else after that.

When Winnie had finally awoken again it was to find her mother and sister at her bedside, the doctor having just gone. Her worst fears had been confirmed, but then the darkness had already been haunted by her nightmares. What difference did it make to know them with her eyes open or shut?

But that wasn't the worst of it. That came later. The absence of Julia was so much more painful than the loss of her because it kept coming. When Winnie thought she had at last regained some peace, something would remind her of the baby she had lost, and she crumpled once more.

Philip.

Philip had been the last thing she'd been able to stand before she let the darkness overcome her.

It had taken her a week to leave her bed, and two more days to gain the courage to break off the engagement. Still, she had been a coward. Finding him alone in the dark only to run away from him once she'd delivered the blow.

"Genevieve truly came to see me?" Winnie finally whispered, her mind probing the darkness she had thought had been unbending.

"Many times. She was a very persistent young lady." Mathilda squeezed her hand, and Winnie thought of all the times she had done that before.

Mathilda had been with Winnie since she was a baby herself. Mathilda was in some of her earliest memories. She had been younger then, of course, but so had Winnie. She squeezed the woman's hand in return, suddenly feeling the weight of time press down on her.

"Except the earl. Greylock. He did not come." Mathilda turned her head. "He did not come because you asked him not to. Remember you told me as much?"

Winnie did remember, and she could only nod.

Mathilda made a noise deep in her throat that Winnie knew meant the woman approved of something. "That earl is a good man. One can tell."

Winnie turned her head at this to look at her maid. "What do you mean?"

Mathilda kept her eyes forward as she said, "When you asked me to see to him once more, only so many weeks ago, he had only a smile on his face and this light in his eyes." Finally Mathilda looked at her. "It is a good man who doesn't lose that light even when someone gives him every reason to."

The maid said nothing more and instead gained her feet, finding the chemise and stockings she must have discarded on Winnie's dressing table. Winnie watched her going about the room, putting it to rights for the night, wondering at the maid's words.

Had Genevieve truly come to see her in those dark times? Had Winnie refused her friend? Had Genevieve let their friendship go because of Winnie's actions? Had Winnie been wrong all along?

What else then had she been wrong about?

She wasn't sure how long she sat there until Mathilda cleared her throat loudly, and Winnie looked up to see her standing by the door, her arms full of laundry.

"My lady, if I may be so bold. I have a request if you please."

Winnie stood up, keeping her hand wrapped about the post, her fingers idly tracing the twining vines carved into the dark wood. "Yes, Mathilda. Anything at all."

Mathilda ducked her head, appearing almost sheepish, and Winnie felt a wave of apprehension at the woman's obvious discomfort as Mathilda had never shown discomfort before.

Finally she looked up and said, "If you please, my lady, I should prefer it if we were to speak in English from now on. If I am to be the lady's maid to a marchioness, I should like to practice."

Winnie's lips parted as she realized they had been speaking in Norwegian. It came so naturally to her, the round sounds of the language as familiar to her as the sharper ones of English. She'd been speaking Norwegian with Mathilda since she was a babe, and it was no wonder she slipped back into the language when it was just them.

But Mathilda was right. She would be a lady's maid to a marchioness soon, and she should speak English, especially amongst the marquess's household staff. It was only proper.

Winnie swallowed. "Yes, of course Mathilda," she said in English. "I shall try to remember that." She smiled and bid the woman good night, but she didn't sleep. Not for a very long time.

Because for the first time, her plan was suddenly not so clear. There was Mathilda and Philip and her sister, and they were all crowding together in her mind.

Suddenly her punishment wasn't the absolute thing she had thought it to be. She saw that now. But was it enough to change her mind? Certainly not. Not when it came to her sister's happiness.

* * *

IT TOOK Philip more than a week to get his affairs in order.

He had hoped to leave before the end of the week, not knowing when the Lowes planned to arrive in Sutton Cross and wishing to get there ahead of them. But it had taken him longer than planned to organize everything.

For one, there was Grandmother Regina. He knew the woman was sometimes forgetful, but her tenacity had never wavered, and it had taken a good deal of convincing on his part to get her to agree to Sutton Cross over Bath. He wanted to feel guilty for the subterfuge, but if there was one thing Grandmother Regina enjoyed, it was trying new things. As Sutton Cross was the latest fashionable spa town, or that was what the rumors would suggest, rumors Philip thought were likely started by Chichester himself, Grandmother Regina had been more than happy to go along with his suggestion once he'd explained what Sutton Cross was.

She too was overly excited to stay in a hotel with over one

hundred rooms. Philip couldn't help but think how well the woman would get along with Lord Bibury.

He had left the rest to Aunt Verity who would be joining them as Grandmother's companion. They were to close the house in Grosvenor Square as Philip hadn't any idea how long they would be in Sutton Cross, but as the season was drawing to a close in London, he thought the Lowes would have no reason to rush back. He wanted to make sure everything was settled for an extended stay.

Philip met with his solicitors and sent word to his man of affairs about his plans. While Philip was not yet the marquess himself, he found his father had lost interest in the title's business long ago, and when Philip had come of age and as the Earl of Greylock, he had found the title in rather sore shape. It had only taken a little attention on his part to have the estates running again, but he wouldn't let them flounder now with his bold plan to chase a woman to Norfolk.

He checked himself. He wasn't really chasing her. He was taking Grandmother Regina to partake of the healing waters as a loyal grandson would do.

He cringed as he blotted his signature on the last letter he had to write that afternoon. A spa town in Norfolk? And Sutton Cross no less. Philip wasn't sure what it was he would find there, but he had a terrible feeling Grandmother Regina would be disappointed and demand to be taken directly to Bath upon departure to experience a real spa town.

He was surprised when a knock came at the door of his study, and he looked up, expecting to see Sheldon, the Hodge House butler, but the door remained closed. He knew his mother was in her rooms as she usually was at that hour, and his father was at his club. That meant...

"Enter," he called and relaxed back in his chair, bracing himself for the worst.

Caroline strode in, arms flung wide as she said, "I'm to be married. Congratulate me."

"Hawk finally made up his mind, did he?"

Caroline dropped her arms, disappointment marring her features. "How did you know it was him?"

Philip laughed and stood. He went to his sister and planted a kiss on her cheek.

"Congratulations, sister," he said. "You and Hawk will make each other perfectly miserable."

"Philip," she chided.

But he only ignored her and returned to his desk, noting the relief that filled him at his sister's announcement. "I'm sorry to spoil your fun, but the last time I saw Hawk was at Grandmother Regina's dinner almost a fortnight ago, and he appeared as though he'd swallowed an entire bottle of cod liver oil."

Caroline sauntered up to his desk and skimmed a hand along one edge before plopping into the chair in front of it. "I hardly think cod liver oil is called for."

Philip finished folding the letter he had written and reached for the sealing wax. "I think it's perfectly in order. You would almost think he had gotten you with child." He pressed his seal into the hot wax on the letter, so he didn't notice Caroline's expression go blank at first. He set down the seal. "He didn't," he said. And when Caroline didn't answer, he pushed to his feet. "I'll kill him."

Caroline shot to her feet and headed him off before he could reach the door. He was surprised by how cool he felt. He thought he would feel more rage toward his friend for violating his sister, but he was oddly in control. Perhaps too much control.

Caroline pushed against his chest with both hands. "Philip, really. This is uncalled for. It isn't Hawk's fault."

"It isn't?" He didn't stop. He enjoyed the sight of her

struggling to keep him at bay far too much. "I suppose you're the victim of immaculate conception then."

She let go suddenly to plant her fists on her hips, and he was forced to catch himself against the chair she'd just vacated. "I'll have you know it was me who seduced him."

He felt his lunch roll over in his stomach. "Caroline, you're my sister. Don't ever say the word seduced again."

Caroline shrugged and this time resumed her seat with a practiced, ladylike flair. "I'll say whatever I wish, Philip. You know that."

He leaned against the desk and eyed her. "And here I thought you were so concerned that Hawk should ruin me when really you were busy ruining him."

She tried to appear innocent, but the look simply wasn't for her. "I think you're to blame actually. If it weren't for my undying love for my dear brother, I wouldn't have been put into this position."

"When is the wedding?" He ignored her pouting, but really he was more interested in learning when it was she would vacate Hodge House. The sooner she was away from their parents the better.

She grew serious almost immediately, the act dropping as she came to her feet. "That's why I'm here actually. Hawk would like to be married as soon as possible, considering..." She let her eyes drop but did not state what she likely knew they were both thinking. "And Audrey tells me you're leaving London. She said something about taking Grandmother Regina to a spa town." She shook her head. "Why on earth are you going to Bath?"

He straightened to go back around his desk and resume his seat, sorting through the piles of correspondence there. "I'm not going to Bath. We're going to Sutton Cross."

She put her hands to her hips once more. "Sutton Cross? Wherever is that?"

"Norfolk."

She looked about the desk as if searching for an answer there. "Norfolk? I've never heard of such a thing."

"It's the Marquess of Chichester's new venture. He's apparently erected a hotel there and everything. I'm taking Grandmother Regina for a respite."

"The Marquess of Chichester?" He didn't miss the note of question in Caroline's voice and looked up as she perched on the guest chair, leaning forward so she was forced to place one hand on his desk. "I thought the Marquess of Chichester was to be married. To someone we know." Her tone turned ominous then, and she tilted her head down to pin him with her glare.

"There isn't a formal engagement yet."

Caroline's eyebrows shot up. "Philip," she breathed and then looked about the room again. "How long was I gone? When did you develop such a backbone?"

He frowned. "You were gone?"

Her expression could have frozen fire. "I was going to ask you not to tell Mother and Father about my current predicament, but it seems there may not be a need." She moved as if to stand before sinking back into her chair. "You really didn't notice I was gone?"

Philip shrugged. "I just thought you were staying with Audrey for a while." A wave of brotherly guilt passed over him. In truth, he was always relieved when his sister left Hodge House. The reasons for such a departure were never important to him as long as she was safe. "Why? Where were you actually?"

Caroline waved him off. "It doesn't matter. What matters is why are you going to Sutton Cross?"

"I told you. I'm taking Grandmother Regina. She expressed a desire to partake of the waters, and so I am escorting her and Aunt Verity to Sutton Cross. It's all perfectly reasonable."

"And will the Lowes be in attendance?"

He kept his gaze on the papers he stacked on his desk. "Perhaps. Winnie might have mentioned something of it."

Caroline surged to her feet again, both hands planted on the desk now as she leaned toward him. "Winnie? I thought you said she wouldn't speak to you."

He held up a finger. "Mathilda wouldn't let me in to speak with her, so I made other arrangements."

"Philip!" Caroline nearly cried, coming around the desk to poke him in the shoulder. "You saw Winnie and said nothing of it to me?"

He leaned back in his chair and pressed his fingertips together. "You just told me you haven't been here."

"But you didn't know that." She tilted her head in response.

He swallowed. "Very well. It's just that things have been moving rather quickly over the past several weeks, and I'm only just now gathering myself."

"To leave."

"Yes, to leave." He poked her in the shoulder this time. "When is the wedding? I promise to be back."

"Hawk is hoping to have the license by the end of the month."

Four weeks. That left him four weeks to discover why Winnie was so adamant to marry the Marquess of Chichester. He stood and held out his hand. "I promise to return before the month is out. You have my word."

She eyed his hand as if it were a venomous snake, but finally she took it, and they shook. "You wouldn't go back on your word, would you?"

"Never." He nodded at the desk. "Now get out of my way. I'm trying to get things in order so I can leave."

Caroline hesitated for only the smallest of moments, her gaze narrowed, before seeming to reach some kind of conclusion. She was several paces away from the desk when she turned back around.

"Philip? Does Winnie know you're going to Sutton Cross too?"

He placed the letters that were to go out that day in a separate pile from the correspondence for his solicitors. "No, I shouldn't think so." He looked up. "But she told me she's in a bit of a predicament with her sister. You remember Ingrid, don't you?"

Caroline gave a nod. "What kind of predicament?"

"I'm afraid she isn't showing well, and this is her first season. Winnie is trying her best to have the girl appear to her advantage, but it seems to not be working. I thought I might be able to help."

Caroline spoke carefully then, more carefully than he had ever heard her before, and he set down the rest of the post still in hand to give her his full attention. "Did she ask you for help, Philip? Or are you simply giving it of your own accord?"

He considered her question before shrugging. "Does it matter?"

"Well, I rather think it does. Some people don't wish for help for one thing, but I've known you a very long time, brother, and I know sometimes you are truly helpful. But I also know sometimes when you wish to provide help, it's really more about ensuring a situation turns out how you wish it to. Which one is it this time?"

He crossed his arms over his chest, feeling his muscles tighten in defense. "When have I ever tried to control the outcome of a situation?"

Her smile was soft, if not a touch sad, and he felt the defensiveness strengthen to something like self-preservation.

She shook her head slowly. "It needn't matter, Philip. Just think about what I've said." She was almost to the door when she stopped again and looked over her shoulder. "One other thing. Was it your idea to go to a spa town or someone else's?"

The line had reappeared between her brows, and Philip dropped his arms as he said, "It was Grandmother Regina's actually. Why?"

She shook her head again. "No reason," she said and left.

CHAPTER 8

"This wasn't precisely what I had in mind when you said we were going to a spa town, Mother." Winnie's father was most likely voicing the thing everyone else was thinking at that moment.

It was rather obvious from the start that when Chichester had said the hotel was ready for visitors, he meant this in the most basic way. Tradesmen still littered the outside of the edifice, scaffolding marking one side, carts blocking the roadway as workers bustled about. And the hotel wasn't the only building under construction.

There was an entire row of shops having a new walkway installed, their doors hampered by planks of wood and buckets of nails, workers shouting orders back and forth to one another. They had seen a team on the outskirts of town even grading the roads. Perhaps Chichester had been rather optimistic when he said the hotel would be open for visitors when he did. But they were there, and they would make the best of it. She was determined.

If only the rain would let up.

"I've never before worried about drowning on dry land,

but I must say I'm thinking of it now," Father muttered, his eyes fixed out the window.

Her father's worry was not unfounded. The rain had started shortly after they'd left the inn in King's Lynn that morning, and it had only increased since then. The fact that the roads were not properly graded yet had Winnie more concerned that their carriage would become affixed to the road until proper drainage could be attained.

As it was, they were waiting in a long line of such carriages before the hotel door as guests alighted for what was to be the grand opening week at the Hotel Sutton Cross, the spa town's premier accommodations.

It was in the sudden stillness that her worries renewed their grip on her. Somehow her simple plan had grown tentacles that seemed to be wiggling their way into all parts of her life, and she did not care for it. She couldn't allow anything to work its way into her resolve, especially not when it concerned another member of her family. And Mathilda was family.

But no matter how she tried she couldn't stop replaying their conversation from that night when Mathilda had asked her to speak in English. A little piece of Winnie's heart broke at the thought. She'd been speaking Norwegian with Mathilda all her life. How different it would be to hear the woman's beautiful voice be wasted on the hard sounds of a different language. It would change something certainly, and it was something Winnie wasn't sure she wished to give up. The melodic round sounds of Mathilda speaking Norwegian were the foundation of so many childhood memories. To have it suddenly disappear because Winnie must marry a marquess seemed unbelievable.

She raised her chin and pushed herself deeper into her seat. She couldn't let thoughts of Mathilda sway her.

Or thoughts of Philip.

Lud, when had everything grown so complicated?

She looked back out the window, hoping to find they had moved, but they were still stopped where they had been, the haberdashery opposite them a watery blur through the pane.

She had left Philip safely back in London, and she wouldn't give him another precious thought. Not about how he had danced with Ingrid or how he'd sat next to her and held her hand in his while he shared a memory with her that only the two of them could have understood, and how—

"What do you think of it, Father?" Winnie asked, forcing her voice to be even and calm, as she leaned forward to once again look out the window she shared with her father.

"The stucco's rotting," he muttered.

Winnie squinted through the rain. "How can you tell?" The hotel was little more than a blur between the scaffolding and the torrential downpour.

"Did Chichester say if he purchased an existing building to renovate? I would have thought he'd build a new one for modern accommodations." Her father leaned closer to the glass.

Winnie swallowed. "He didn't say actually."

This wasn't the first time her father had voiced a concern over one of Chichester's real estate ventures. The first had been a public room in Belgravia that served chalked milk. Chichester had claimed not to know of the practice, but Winnie was never sure.

"Would a building in Norfolk have been erected using stucco? I would think that was a more Mediterranean style." She tried to look where her father was scanning the building but didn't know exactly what she was looking for.

He leaned back as if he'd seen enough. "Its architect may have employed stucco if his design was of the Italianate style." Father shrugged. "It doesn't matter really. If the original building was erected with the stuff, it should have been repaired during renovations. Especially with such visible deterioration."

"Do try to be positive, Carl," Winnie's mother said from behind her newspaper. "We're supposed to be encouraging, remember?"

Her father slid Winnie a glance then, and she couldn't help but feel a sting at the flatness she saw there. While her mother had understood Winnie's reasons for trying to secure Chichester's hand, she was afraid her father had never truly understood it. The title he had unexpectedly inherited still made little sense to him. He was more at home in a pile of books and blueprints than in the middle of a society ball or God forbid, in the throes of matchmaking schemes.

"I am always positive, Ada," he said, but he wiggled his eyebrows as he did so, and Winnie and Ingrid did all they could to stifle a giggle as their mother dropped her newspaper to her lap in obvious suspicion.

Winnie's father was saved from further reprimand when their carriage pulled to the front of the line at the hotel. Their tiger didn't bother dropping the step as it would have simply sunk in the mud, so instead her father alighted first, proving the truth of their theory when he sank into the mud up to his ankles.

Ingrid recoiled at the sight of her father's sunken boots while Mother raised an eyebrow and shook her head.

"There's nothing to be done for it I'm afraid." She leaned forward on the bench and tossed the newspaper aside. "Carl, turn around, dear."

Winnie's father was a tall man, which meant he was an excellent fit for Mother's statuesque size, but there had never been a time when Winnie was so glad for her father's stature. Mother braced herself with a hand on either side of the door as Ingrid scrambled back on her seat.

"Mother, what are you doing?"

Mother glanced at her youngest daughter briefly. "I can't very well walk into the hotel, child. I would be rendered unpresentable in a moment." She reached one hand through the door to Father's shoulder just as Ingrid exclaimed.

"Mother, what if the Clarkes should see you?"

Mother sighed and once again turned to her youngest daughter. "No one will be stopping to take in the view in this weather, dear." And with that, she launched herself out the door and onto Father's back.

Winnie sucked in a breath as her father took the brunt of Mother's weight. He stumbled once, twice, before catching both of his wife's legs in his hands and setting off through the rain in the direction of the hotel.

The main entrance was sheltered by a portico, but it did little so far as protecting the incoming guests as the rain had begun to fall sideways. The wind had picked up somewhere along the way, and it tore at the footmen's jackets as they tried to pull luggage from the carriages in line. Mother was quite right. There was nothing to be done about it.

Winnie leaned forward, taking in the depth of the muddy footprints her father had left. Their gowns would be ruined in an instant should they try to walk to the hotel. And what if Chichester should see her then? Surely on the opening day of his hotel he would be waiting in the lobby to receive his guests. What would he think if she appeared half-drowned and as though she'd had a tumble in a barn yard no less? No, her mother had been right. They must wait for Father to retrieve them.

"Oh Winnie, my hat," Ingrid whined, holding a delicate hand to the new bonnet her sister had purchased just before they left London. It was a beautiful rendering of lavender and springs of dried gypsophila, and it would be utterly destroyed in the rain.

Winnie bent toward the door again in search of her father's return.

"Perhaps Father can—" She didn't finish the sentence. She screamed instead. "Philip!"

His name was lost in the roar of the rain, but he smiled as though he heard her perfectly. He bent inside the carriage and reached for Ingrid.

"Here. Put this round your shoulders and pull the hood over your bonnet to protect it," he said, and Winnie realized he was handing her sister a cloak.

Her sister did as he bid, pulling the hood of the cloak gently over her bonnet. Unlike her father, Philip reached into the carriage and pulled Ingrid into his arms. Her willowy sister was dwarfed by Philip's bulk, and he carried her easily through the mud to the front of the hotel where he deposited her within the shelter of the building.

Winnie watched as he helped Ingrid from the cloak and waited while her sister disappeared inside, caught up in a gaggle of other arriving guests.

When Philip turned back to her, his gaze meeting hers through the rain, Winnie could admit her heart skipped in her chest. She had watched him the whole time he carried her sister, and her body responded at the mere suggestion in his gaze.

He was going to do the same to her, but somehow she knew he wouldn't hold her with such careful, objective reserve. The rain sluiced from the brim of his hat, the shoulders of his greatcoat glistening with the damp, and her heart thundered as her stomach tightened.

She wanted him to touch her.

Like in the maze when she'd grabbed him, and he'd grabbed her. Like that night in the retiring room when they'd touched hands and touched each other's souls. Like before…

She should have been wondering what he was doing there instead of allowing her thoughts to stray to such dangerous topics, but she couldn't have forced a practical thought through her mind just then if it were a matter of life and death.

This time when he came to the carriage door, he didn't speak. He wordlessly held out the cloak, and she slipped it on, pulling the hood over her head. The cloak was bigger on her than on her sister, and she found herself getting lost in the folds of fabric that had grown wet even in the short walk to the hotel's door.

Philip's arms came around her before she was ready, but it was better that way. It was better that she didn't have time to think about his hard body, about the impossible heat that exuded from him as his arms closed around her, as she found herself braced against his incredibly broad, hard chest.

He had carried her sister to the door and returned in a matter of seconds, but when he held her, time seemed to stretch, and she willed it to keep slowing. In the shelter of Philip's arms, everything was all right. Ingrid could marry Robert, and Mathilda could keep speaking Norwegian. None of it had to change, and yet everything could.

But then Philip set her down all too quickly, and she was forced to find her footing on the uneven wooden boards of the small walkway bordering the hotel. It took her a moment to figure out where he had placed her as the hotel door was nowhere in sight. She was forced to push back the hood just enough to see a group of guests had beat them to the door and were now arguing with a line of footmen trying to get luggage through the same door. It was rather a disaster that was not helped by the driving rain finding its way under the portico.

Except she didn't feel the rain. She looked up and around and realized Philip had brought them under the scaffolding.

They were shielded on one side by a canvas tarp hanging from the wooden beams as well as the reach of the portico. She could still feel the damp in the air, and the wind pulled at the hood of the cloak, but she was far safer than the melee of gentlemen and ladies struggling to breach the door at the same time as the footmen with their piles of luggage.

It was then, in the shadows of the scaffolding, that she realized Philip still held her, and she looked up, her breath catching at the heat in his green eyes.

His hands had slipped from her shoulders and disappeared beneath the cloak, finding their way to the dip just above her hips and settling there. She laid her hands delicately on his chest, almost afraid to touch him, that if she did, it would cause something to happen like a spark of flint against fiber. In her mind she saw the spiral of it, the tentacles trying to worm their way into her plan, spiraling deeper.

But she had to touch him. Just a little. Just enough.

It would never be enough.

And then Philip's hands curled into her, his grip tightening, and she felt the desire that simmered between them, the thing that remained unspoken, but his grip on her said everything that needed to be said.

Mine.

The breath caught in the back of her throat, and her lips parted. She couldn't look away though. She couldn't breathe. She couldn't move because if she did this moment might end, and suddenly she wanted to see what Philip would do, see how far he would go.

Would it be far enough?

Far enough to save her?

The crash of an overturned luggage cart brought her back to reality, and her heart stuttered in fear at how reckless she was, how daring, how stupid, how *weak*.

She stepped back too quickly, the stucco of the hotel wall

biting into her back, but Philip had already let go, and something died inside of her.

She was running, pulling the cloak from her shoulders and tossing it back at him. She pushed her way through the hotel doors before she left what remained of her heart out in the rain.

* * *

HE HAD MADE A MISTAKE.

He knew that now, standing in the line of guests trying to enter the grand ballroom that night for the opening assembly. The smell of sweat from the crowded bodies and the sooty aroma of the thousands of candles lit in the chandeliers above served to quell any desire that had shot through him at the sensation of holding Winnie against him.

Not to mention he was currently escorting his grandmother in her Bath chair. The presence of one's grandmother did have a dampening effect on one's lust.

He leaned forward so Grandmother Regina could hear him. "How are you, Grandmother? You're not finding tonight's gaiety to be too much?"

Grandmother Regina raised a gloved hand to wave him away before he'd even finished speaking. "Hush up, boy. I'm trying to hear what everyone is saying. Is it true there is a bath house here?"

Aunt Verity adjusted her wrap more snuggly against her as she said, "Yes, Mother, there is a grand bath house by the spring. Should you like to see it?"

Philip didn't miss the way Aunt Verity's mouth tightened at her words, and he suddenly wondered how exhausting it must be to care for his grandmother. Aunt Verity's disposition was pleasant, and she tended to be an optimist. But it was the physical aspects of caring for a woman who had suffered such a debilitating stroke that Philip suddenly realized must be taxing on a slight woman like his aunt.

"I shall be happy to escort you there, Grandmother. You must only say the word," he said.

Aunt Verity looked sharply at him, her eyes wide, her lips slightly parted, and he felt like the worst cad for not offering to help his aunt sooner.

It had been several years since Grandmother Regina's stroke, and Aunt Eugenia, Ethan's mother and Grandmother Regina's eldest daughter, had decided Aunt Verity should be her caregiver. No one in the family had voiced an objection, one rarely did with Aunt Eugenia, and Philip was beginning to understand the fault in such decision-making. He would speak to Ethan about it upon his return. If there was anyone who could reign in Aunt Eugenia, it was her eldest son.

The line began to move then, and Philip heard the distant plucking of a violin and cello and knew the music must be starting, people filtering onto the dance floor and opening space around the ballroom for more guests to enter. He wrapped his hands more securely around Grandmother Regina's chair and began the slow trek into the room.

He didn't look around for Winnie. He knew the moment she had a chance she would confront him. He'd nearly ravished her right there against the side of the building, in the pouring rain no less. He hesitated, but he could no longer hear the sound of the unending rain over the chatter of guests and the overtures of music. But he could feel it. How rain had a way of closing things in, making them cozier than they actually were, presenting a false sense of intimacy that wasn't there.

That was why he'd almost kissed her, out there in plain sight. Chichester could have seen them, and this whole ordeal would have been over.

Only he hadn't kissed her.

He had only just been able to hold himself back, Hawk's words pinging through his head.

But what if Hawk were wrong?

That day at the bridge dedication seemed so long ago now. Had he been so sure then of her resolve to marry Chichester? Had he been so sure she was telling the truth when she said she loved the marquess?

He didn't know now. It was easy to convince someone of a lie, but actions didn't lie. He had felt the way her hips pressed into him at his touch, so subtle, almost imperceptible, and yet it had told him so much. He wasn't even sure she'd realized she had done it. She likely wasn't aware, her body betraying her when her mind had tried to remain steadfast.

He wasn't so sure now of his plan. Was it truly his best option to persuade Chichester to his friendship and into his confidence? Philip didn't think so. He'd seen a chink in Winnie's armor, and he was desperate enough to exploit it.

He had just settled Grandmother Regina's Bath chair along the side of the dance floor where she could watch the young people as they twirled and bowed when Lord Bibury emerged from the crowd, unlit cigar in one hand and his wife in the other.

"Greylock!" he called above the din.

Lady Bibury smiled as her husband pulled her along. She greeted Aunt Verity and Grandmother Regina in turn as Lord Bibury pointed at the assembled guests.

"Can you believe this, Greylock? In Norfolk, no less?"

Philip nodded. "It seems a rather odd place for a spa town, doesn't it? I would think Norfolk would attract more visitors for its shoreline and salt marshes."

"I said the very same thing," Bibury said. "But Ada insisted we come."

Philip looked past Bibury to find Winnie stepping up to

their group with her sister. He saw the moment she spotted Grandmother Regina, her eyes widening in recognition before her gaze flew to him.

He smiled as he said, "Yes, I felt the same when Grandmother Regina suggested we take in the waters." He spoke loud enough for Winnie to hear him, and he watched as she bit her lip in consternation.

If she had wondered if he'd followed her there, he had just given her evidence to unsettle her conclusions. Even if he had been influential in Grandmother's sudden decision to travel to Sutton Cross, it did not negate the fact that it had been his grandmother's idea in the first instance.

"Lady Winnaretta. Lady Ingrid." He bowed to the Lowe daughters as was proper and again to Lady Bibury as she finished greeting his grandmother and aunt. "I hope you are finding the evening's entertainment to be to your liking."

Ingrid wrinkled her nose almost immediately. "It would be lovely if there weren't so much…dancing."

Philip's toes smarted as if in memory, and he reached into his coat. "About that, Lady Ingrid. I hope it isn't too forward of me, but I procured something for you in London." He withdrew his hand and extended the item to Ingrid as the rest of their group watched. He was particularly aware of Winnie's gaze, and he hated how suspicious it was. "I thought this may aid you in your attempts at dancing."

Ingrid accepted his gift and held it with both hands, a line appearing between her brows in confusion. "A fan?" She spread the thing open, and understanding dawned as her eyes widened, but it was Winnie's sharp intake of breath that made him smile.

"It contains the steps to the quadrille on one side and the steps to the cotillion on the other. I thought you might find it useful."

"I say," Lord Bibury commented. "I didn't know such a thing existed."

"Oh, it does," Philip assured him. "My sister was given one before." He smiled, laughter warming his voice as he remembered his sister learning to dance. "You know how Caroline is. She is quite enthusiastic about any endeavor she undertakes. Sometimes she can be too enthusiastic."

Lady Bibury laughed and reached for the fan to examine it. "How extraordinary." She looked to her older daughter. "Why didn't we think to acquire one of these when the season started?"

Winnie looked at Philip when she answered. "I suppose I didn't think of it as I've never had need of one before."

There was something about her gaze that unsettled him, but he couldn't piece it together just then. It wasn't distaste he saw there or opposition. It was something more complicated than that. Almost as if Winnie didn't wish to feel…gratitude toward his gift.

He met her gaze, trying to assure her with his own that there was no other motive for his gift. He had experienced firsthand the devastation Ingrid could inflict with her feet, and his only wish was to prevent other unsuspecting victims from suffering the same fate.

The dance ended then, the music coming to a flourishing end, and the crowd shifted about them as dancers swapped partners, preparing for the next set.

Lord Bibury stepped up and bowed to Aunt Verity. "Lady Verity, I should be honored if you would partner me for the next dance."

Aunt Verity didn't speak, her face showing her astonishment as she looked to Lady Bibury for help, but Lady Bibury only waved her off.

"Oh, do indulge him, Lady Verity. I should like to catch up with my dearest Regina." Lady Bibury patted Regina's hand.

"Did you take in the Rossi Exhibition at the Marlborough? Simply scandalous, wasn't it?"

Grandmother Regina raised her eyebrows. "Oh, it was a lovely exhibition." She leaned forward as if imparting a terrible secret. "Italian men must be built differently than English ones. I've never seen an Englishmen who looks anything like Rossi's statues." Grandmother widened her eyes as if to convey her meaning, and Lady Bibury patted her hand with glee, leaning in for further gossip as Lord Bibury took Aunt Verity's arm to lead her onto the dance floor.

He turned back at the last moment to Philip. "Perhaps you could partner Lady Winnaretta for this dance, Greylock."

"Father," Winnie said sharply, but the man only smiled and walked out to the dance floor.

Philip smiled and offered his arm to Winnie. "Perhaps a promenade then?"

Winnie turned away, and he realized she was looking to her sister for help, but Ingrid had floated away toward a pair of debutantes currently clustered around the punch bowl.

Winnie frowned. "I suppose a promenade will be all right," she muttered.

They had made it a quarter of the way about the room before Winnie spoke again. "I should like to have a private conversation with you, Lord Greylock."

Her voice was pitched low, but he very much thought the din of excitement around them was enough to cover any speech they may have.

He knew this would be coming, but hearing her speak the words as though he were due a scolding had his mood souring. "I had a feeling you would. Might I suggest the lobby? There's a—"

"A private conversation, Philip," she all but hissed now, and Philip knew he was not going to win this battle.

They had reached the far side of the ballroom where tall

windows looked out over what must have been a manicured garden but at that hour offered little more than their reflections. Winnie paused, causing him to tug at her arm, and he realized she was peering about them, taking in the guests.

He realized too late what she had done. She had brought them to a corner of the room far removed from anyone's attention, and before he could properly formulate what she was about to do, she gave his arm a great tug, pulling him into the shadows.

"Winnie, I think—"

"Shhh," she hissed, pulling on his arm with more ferocity.

They tumbled through an archway he hadn't seen before and plunged into an all but black corridor. He gathered the sense of plaster walls and marble floors about them, but he could not see anything of marked distinction.

"Winnie, I should ask you to have a care for my reputation."

She made a noise then that made him wish he could see her face in the darkness. She still had hold of his arm though, and she began pulling again. He wondered briefly if she knew where they were going, and this only served to send a white-hot flash of jealousy through him.

Had Chichester given her a private tour then? Philip had spotted the man as soon as he'd entered the lobby earlier. The marquess played the consummate host well, oiled and polished to hide all the cracks. Was Winnie now familiar with all of the dark, quiet places of the Hotel Sutton Cross? He saw red at just the idea.

But then she tripped, and if their arms hadn't been intertwined, she would have fallen. As it was, he had to reach out his free hand to steady her. He caught her, holding her a touch longer than he needed to, but the sudden smell of overwhelming damp penetrated his senses.

"Winnie, where…"

He didn't finish the sentence. Because whatever Winnie had tripped over had not been affixed to the floor and just then it fell with a resounding crash that reverberated down the corridor, letting everyone in attendance at the grand opening of the Hotel Sutton Cross know just exactly where they were.

CHAPTER 9

Winnie froze, a torrent of possibilities cascading through her mind as the crash reverberated around them. None of them good.

Chichester discovering them. Chichester asking her for an explanation. Having to explain—

What exactly?

She didn't understand what was happening between her and Philip—although she would argue nothing was, even as she felt it for the lie it was—nor how Chichester might react. The man had remained so aloof when he interacted with her. It was as though she were just another person to whom he relayed his many and varied believed accomplishments.

Suddenly standing there in the near dark with Philip, the rest of her life with Chichester seemed very long indeed.

Near dark?

She swung about toward the shaft of light that had appeared in the wall next to them. Whatever it was she had crashed into had apparently gone through the wall as it toppled over. For a moment, fear lodged in her throat. How was she to explain this? Destruction of Chichester's property?

But then—

The noise still sounded in her ears. Crash after crash, the split of light in the wall flashing with each crash, and Winnie held a hand to her chest, thinking it her heart trying to escape.

But now, it wasn't that. It was…

"Fireworks."

She turned to where she thought Philip was standing in the darkness, and now, thanks to the hole in the wall, she could almost make out his features.

He gestured to the hole she had created. "Fireworks. This must be the same side of the building where the tall windows were in the ballroom. The fireworks can probably be seen through them. I bet Chichester arranged it for tonight's entertainment."

Now that the imminent threat of discovery had receded, Winnie willed her heart to calm enough to listen more carefully, and quickly she picked out a different sound through the cacophony.

Cheers and exclamations of awe.

She rubbed her hands up and down her arms as relief coursed through her. No one was coming to find them. No one had even likely heard them.

Philip moved then, and she almost forgot what she had been doing, luring him away from the assembly. She thought he was trying to escape and reached out a hand for him, which he gripped in his own, pulling her after him. He wasn't trying to escape actually. He was investigating the hole in the wall.

"I think you've uncovered an old doorway." His voice was muffled as he leaned through the opening. He gave a tug of her hand, and she slipped forward, reaching blindly in the dark, unable to make out her feet or where she was stepping. Her hand connected with wood, and she realized she must have knocked over a series of wooden crates, but she didn't have time to think of it because suddenly they were outside.

She felt the drop in temperature first, just slightly as the air was humid with the echo of the day's downpours. The explosion of fireworks was louder here but still dulled by something standing between them and the greater courtyard. She wasn't sure, but it looked as though a garden had been left unattended and taken over the outer edges of the space with a few more resilient vines snaking their way into the area.

Another flash and finally the musty smell that had greeted her clicked with a memory.

"It's a plunge pool," she said before realizing she would speak, and she turned to find Philip studying their surroundings.

"It is," he agreed, his voice soft as if lost in exploration. "Or at least it was once. Nature has almost reclaimed it."

"It must have been a part of the original building at one time, but they've drained it of water." She could make out the oval shape of the small recess, and each flash of light revealed more of the tile work. "Oh, it's beautiful," she breathed.

She let go of his hand without thinking and moved forward, descending the cracked cement steps of the plunge pool to get a closer look at the azure and emerald that circled the rim of it.

"Winnie, be careful." She heard the concern in Philip's voice, but the craftsmanship the light from each explosion of fireworks uncovered was too much, and she moved forward until she stood in the bottom of the empty pool, her gloved fingers reaching for the tiles.

She paused long enough to tug her gloves free so she could touch the stone directly.

"Philip, do come see. It's beautiful."

When she didn't hear him move, she turned to find him standing where she had left him, and when she met his gaze, she realized her mistake in trying to get him alone.

Heat flared in his eyes, but it was something more than that, something darker and truer.

Her arm dropped to her side, unable to hold it up any longer as the strength was sapped from her body at his look.

She expected him to say something, but he only shook his head as he made his way down into the pool. It was shallow with a small ledge running along the diameter about three or four feet up as the pool was meant for soaking in the restorative qualities of the water and not swimming. Philip took the few steps down with a lazy gait, and she watched him, unable to look away.

"Do you remember that day we first met?" he said when he reached the bottom of the pool and stood only a couple of feet in front of her, leaving her to wonder why he hadn't come closer, why he hadn't tried to touch her.

Because she wanted him to touch her.

The realization and the need came at the same time, flashing through her with a heated intensity that scorched.

She licked her lips and nodded. "Of course I do."

He tilted his head as he took the smallest of steps closer to her. "You had that same look on your face."

"What look?" she all but whispered, his nearness confusing her senses.

She had thought herself recovered from their earlier encounter. She had thought she had firmed her resolve, given herself the lecture she needed to remind herself why she was there, what she was doing, and what was important. But she wasn't. She wasn't recovered at all, and her heart sped up, her hands almost shaking.

"As though you can't believe there's such beauty in the world."

She swallowed now, willed her heart to slow, even as she wished—so ardently wished—he would step closer, that he would touch her again, like he had that afternoon. Only now she wanted more.

More.

She raised her chin, sucked in a breath. "Philip, what are you doing here?"

His grin was slow. "You brought me here, or have you forgotten?"

She wrung her hands together. "I don't mean here here. I mean—" She licked her lips and met his gaze. "You know what I mean."

He was closer now. She hadn't seen him move. It was something subtler than that, more instinctual, and her stomach tightened in anticipation.

"You know why I'm here, Winnie." His voice had turned softer, gravelly.

"I told you, Philip. I love Chichester, and I—"

"No, you don't."

The air caught in her throat. "Are you calling me a liar?"

He shook his head. He was impossibly close now. She could feel the heat emanating from him, and she wanted to sink into it.

"You don't mean to lie. I know that."

"How do you know?"

Finally he touched her. A single finger along the curve of her cheek. It wasn't enough. It was too much. It only served to make her want him more, and she hated it.

"You're trying to convince yourself you love him," he said then, dropping his hand back to his side, and his eyes studied her face, searching. "The only thing is I can't figure out why."

"Philip." It wasn't an answer. It wasn't an explanation. It

was a plea, one she hadn't meant to make, but he seemed to understand.

This time when he lifted his hands, he cupped her face, rested his forehead against hers, and she had to grip his wrists in order to stop herself from going into his arms.

"Tell me," he whispered, his lips nearly touching hers. "Tell me what's wrong, so I can help."

"You can't fix this," she said and kissed him before he could say anything else.

Suddenly she didn't want to hear words. She didn't want him to help. Philip was always helping, but she didn't want that now. Now she wanted just him. She wanted to *feel* just him.

She wanted to forget about the Clarkes and her sister, about Chichester and the engagement. She wanted to forget it all and remember what it was like to just be her. To have this. Philip in her arms.

She remembered this.

Their engagement may have started out as an arrangement, but somewhere along the way as they had waited for their special license, she had fallen and so had he. She knew that even if she had never admitted it to herself. It had never gone further than this, kissing furtively in the dark in secret, but she remembered it. The rasp of his stubbled skin against hers, the curl of his fingers into her back, the sense of him, his impossibly broad shoulders overwhelming her until she forgot every other thing that could hurt her.

Everything except who she truly was. Someone who fell in love with another man while she carried her dead lover's baby.

He moved then, shoving the thought from her mind as he shuffled her backward until cement struck the backs of her legs and then he was lifting her, settling her on the bathing ledge so carefully, so effortlessly.

His hands were everywhere as she tried to reach all of him. There was a frantic quality to their movements, desperate and rushed, as if five years of pent-up desire tried to get out all at once.

She wanted to savor it. She wanted to revel in the fact that it was Philip. It was finally Philip touching her again, kissing her, caressing her, holding her.

But there was no time for savoring. That wasn't what this was about. There was something carnal and possessive about their movements as if they had each rediscovered something they'd thought lost forever.

She wanted to touch him. She wanted the heat of his skin beneath her palms. To feel how alive he was, how real he was.

Because she needed it. She needed to know he was really there after so many years. After so long believing she would never touch him again. She needed at least that.

As his lips skimmed her jaw, her cheeks, the spot behind her ear, she worked at his jacket, shoving aside the fabric to find his waistcoat beneath. She didn't bother trying to unbutton it, merely pushing it up to grab fistfuls of his shirt beneath. She tugged, the sound of fabric ripping getting lost in the boom of fireworks somewhere beyond them.

His lips came back to hers, hungry and probing, and she forgot her determination for a moment, his kiss too much to bear. She leaned into him, deepening the kiss, seeking more, and he answered, tilting her head with one hand, changing the angle and bringing her closer.

His other hand explored her, curving over her shoulders down her chest, over her breast. She moaned, willing his hand to stop, to cup her heavy, aching breast, but he didn't, his hand just as searching and needy as hers.

His hand found the hem of her gown just as she yanked his shirt free of his trousers. Her fingers found the hot skin of his back just as his hand touched her calf, skated higher. When his hand closed over the bare skin at the top of her stocking, she cried out, her head going back as she tried to press closer to him.

"Philip, please."

His lips were at her throat now, and he scraped his teeth along the tender lines of her neck. She bucked, her fingers digging into the flesh of his back. She wanted to trace the muscles there, find the changes time had wrought, but she could do no more than hang on as his hand moved higher up her thigh.

She wanted him to linger, to explore her, to reawaken the desire she had thought long dead, but this wasn't about that. This was about something more than that. This was about possession.

Mine.

And she was his. God, help her, no matter the lies she told herself she would always be his.

She pressed her eyes shut. Not because she couldn't take the pleasure, but because she didn't want him to see the tears that had sprung to her eyes.

She clung to him as his hand found her, as his deliberate fingers parted her folds, and—

"Philip." His name was the only thing she knew how to say as his touch pierced directly through her, fire igniting in a flash of explosion.

He wasn't kind. He didn't lazily circle her nub. He didn't give her time to build to climax. He forced her to it, his fingers knowing just how to touch her, just how to bring her to the brink. He gave her no time to relent, no time to change her mind, no time to stop this.

But she didn't want to stop it. She wanted this.

Pressing her fingers into his back, she levered herself against his hand, and he moaned against her neck.

"God, Winnie, I want to be inside of you." His words were too much.

She came apart, bliss spreading through her body like the fireworks taking over the sky. She threw her head back, her fingernails biting into his flesh, as she let the euphoria of her orgasm overtake her, and for one moment, just one, she let herself be.

* * *

THE FIREWORKS HAD STOPPED.

It was the first thing she realized when she finally roused, her body slumped against Philip. No, not slumped. He was holding her ever so carefully, his arms wrapped completely about her as though he were afraid she would fall from the plunge pool ledge and shatter like a China teacup.

She didn't think it was possible for her heart to shatter again, but it did. She closed her eyes, willing the moment to last forever, but it couldn't. Especially now that the fireworks had finished. Somehow it had felt as though they were given a reprieve as long as the spectacle carried on. While the rest of the world was lost in the glitter and excitement of fireworks, she and Philip were free to be together.

But the fireworks were over, and it was time to return to reality.

She eased away from him, unable to look at his face. Not because she was ashamed of what she had done, but because she was afraid if she looked at him, she wouldn't want to ever give him up.

When he helped her down from the ledge, she concentrated on fixing her skirts, spending far too much time on them when she knew they were ruined, and she would be required to sneak back to her room before anyone saw her.

Finally, when she knew she could waste no more time, she looked up into those green eyes that haunted her dreams.

"Philip, I'm sorry," she said. It was all she managed before she had to swallow, her throat suddenly dry.

He stepped toward her, his hands raised as if to reassure her, but she stopped him by holding up her own hand.

"Not for this," she said, a small laugh escaping her. "I could never be sorry for this." She licked her lips, suddenly unable to bear his tender gaze on her any longer. "I'm sorry for running away that night in the garden. I was—" The breath stopped in her throat as her heart pounded. "I was scared, and I was hurting, but it was no excuse for what I did. I should have stayed."

The words hung between them, an admission so heavy neither of them reached to pick it up.

She had meant to question him about why he was here in Sutton Cross. She couldn't stop the feeling he had followed her, and his intentions were somehow to stop her engagement to Chichester. But then she had seen Grandmother Regina, and her resolve had wavered. Grandmother Regina had always been so kind to her five years ago, so supportive and encouraging. The woman hadn't known the reason for her grandson's sudden engagement, but she also didn't seem to care. She was just delighted at the idea of a wedding.

Winnie's heart gave a lurch then, and she realized she didn't want to know why Philip had followed because she was afraid it was for the reasons she wished he had followed her.

Because he loved her.

"I'm sorry I walked away that night, and I'm sorry I hurt you." There. The words that had weighed on her for days now—weeks? years?—were finally out. She thought the pressure on her chest would have eased, but it didn't.

Instead she saw the shock on his face at her words, the hope that flared in his eyes, and the heaviness grew unbearable.

She held up both hands now. "That doesn't mean things can change now, Philip. I must marry Chichester. I must, and I'm sorry." She shook her head. "You have no idea how sorry I am." She sucked in a breath, feeling the tears coming and knowing she must leave before she allowed them to spill down her cheeks.

It wasn't that she didn't want Philip to see her cry. It was that she didn't think she could bear it if he tried to comfort her. And he would try. He always had.

He took a step forward, and she held up a hand. "No, Philip." She took a step back, her feet scraping the stone floor of the plunge pool. "It's late, and someone may be looking for me. I'll find my own way back to my rooms. It's probably best we're not seen together."

He opened his mouth, and the urge to run was strong, but she stayed. She waited, giving him time like she had never done before, but he only closed his mouth, his expression one of resignation. He nodded, but he never spoke, and her heart hurt.

"Good night, Philip," she said and then turned to climb from the pool.

She'd reached the broken doorway before he finally spoke.

"Winnie."

She closed her eyes against the sound of her name on his lips. Turning only her head, she looked back at him. He hadn't moved, and he stood in the bottom of the plunge pool, decay and neglect all around him, and she wondered if that weren't an omen for something.

"You know I love you." He stood perfectly still, his arms

loose at his sides, but in his eyes, she saw everything, and it destroyed her.

"I do," she said, but she still slipped through the door and back into the darkness.

CHAPTER 10

$\mathcal{P}$hilip stood in the lobby of the Hotel Sutton Cross the following morning and tried to think of anything else than what had transpired the previous night.

It wasn't the physical aspects of it, even though, God, he could not and *would* not scrub that from his mind. Five years ago he had felt like a thief and her kisses were precious jewels, but last night…hell's teeth, last night. He hadn't felt like he was stealing anything. It was as though he had finally rediscovered something that had been his all along.

His.

It was at that moment that Chichester came down the central staircase surrounded by a bevy of gentlemen Philip suspected were more unwitting investors. Was Chichester ever not scheming?

"Greylock!" Philip winced at the sound of his name as Chichester raised a hand in greeting, stopping at the bottom of the steps to call out. "We'll be seeing you at the fountain shortly, yes?"

Philip forced a smile and raised a hand in return. "Wouldn't miss it!"

Chichester smiled that oily smile that conned old ladies and swindled respectable gentlemen before disappearing through the lobby doors, bedeviled gentlemen in tow.

Jesus.

He couldn't do this. Perhaps Hawk had been wrong. Perhaps Philip needn't befriend the man. Perhaps there still was a way to reach Winnie without having to resort to wheedling his way into the potential fiancé's good graces.

He turned to the row of small windows that dotted that side of the lobby, his gaze lingering on the passing traffic outside, Chichester already gone from view. At least it had stopped raining. The sky hung heavy with gray clouds, but it was somewhat heartening to see that he mustn't stand out in the rain for this.

"Ready, my grandson?"

He turned back at his grandmother's voice. Verity pushed the woman's Bath chair across the lobby, the large wheels whirring across the gleaming marble floors.

"Ah, Grandmother Regina. Aren't you looking simply lovely this morning?"

Grandmother Regina smiled as she said, "Don't patronize me, boy. I once swaddled you. Don't think I can't do it again."

Philip smiled at his grandmother's cheekiness and looked to Aunt Verity, but her gaze was lost somewhere across the lobby. He tried to see where she was looking, but just as he did so, a large group of guests poured from the central staircase in the direction of the doors.

The guests of the hotel had been invited to partake of the waters that morning, and the hotel was emptying in droves as people eager to find restorative powers in a single sip struck out in the direction of the spring.

He attempted to see if Winnie were among them, but the crowd was far too eager and rushed for the doors. He didn't find any members of the Lowe family in what he could see of the group that surged for the door just then.

He couldn't help but wonder if she'd made it back to her room safely. He tried not to overthink the matter, but it was damned difficult not to. He'd spent a sleepless night wondering what it was she could possibly be thinking, of herself, of him, and worst of all, of *them*. Would she try to avoid him? Did she think he would stop now if she but asked it of him?

Did she hate him?

He had told her he loved her. She hadn't rebuked his emotions. No, it was far worse than that. She'd admitted she'd already known of his feelings. God, why had she apologized to him? Why had she made this all so much worse by being the kind, generous person she was?

That night in the garden when Winnie had broken the engagement, she had asked him to give her peace, and he had done just that for five years. He hadn't meant to so blatantly go against her wishes. It had just…happened.

As so many things tended to with Winnie.

He had had their carriage brought around as he worried the roads would be impassable for the Bath chair, but when they emerged from the hotel, he was surprised to see a walkway of sorts had been fashioned from planks of wood leading from the hotel to the high street where Chichester had said a small square held the fountain from which guests could drink of the spring water.

"We were in that carriage for two days, Philip. Please say we might try this walkway." Grandmother Regina indicated the platform, and Philip wondered if Chichester had had men laboring on the thing through the night for it hadn't been there the previous day.

Philip looked to Aunt Verity, but she only shrugged. He switched places with her, and she didn't try to fight him on it. If they were to get Grandmother and her chair up to the high street, it would take a great deal of effort, but he wasn't about to deny the woman such a simple thing.

They fell into place along with the rest of the guests headed toward the spring, and he couldn't help but peer around them looking for any sighting of the Lowes.

"I am so very glad it stopped raining. This would be dreadful in the rain, wouldn't it, pumpkin?"

Philip looked at Aunt Verity who returned his curious gaze. It was difficult to tell whom Grandmother Regina was referring to when she used pet names such as this, but Verity shrugged and said, "Yes, it would have been, Mother."

The high street was thankfully at a slightly higher elevation and most of the previous day's rain had drained from the main thoroughfare, leaving it slightly less muddy than the side road that contained the hotel.

They reached the square much sooner than Philip had thought they would. It was a small space, and rather sad, if he were honest. A crumbling statue of a man in uniform sat in the middle of it, his nose broken off, and his musket sporting a repair that had turned it into a bayonet at the end instead of a musket at all. He almost missed the fountain itself entirely as it was shrunken and obscured by Chichester and his cronies. Philip eyed the thing, wondering how someone could believe it had mystical powers. It looked like he could do nothing more than give a person a serious case of intestinal distress.

He parked Grandmother's Bath chair to the side where it wouldn't be in the way of the other guests wishing to approach the fountain but also would give her a grand view of whatever it was Chichester had up his sleeve, and he was sure it would be quite something. Philip was certain the marquess wouldn't miss the opportunity to tout the many varied and exceptional benefits of the water, but Philip still wasn't convinced the water wasn't brackish.

He realized he was studying the crowd more than the spectacle they had come to see and forced himself to watch Chichester and the fountain and resisted the urge to seek out the Lowes. After all, it was Chichester he was supposed to be wooing, wasn't it?

A cart had been placed next to the fountain, and Philip could see it contained tray upon tray of very small glasses, likely the very glasses the guests were supposed to use to sample the water. It seemed Chichester was keen to share the alluring water with his guests, just not too much of it.

Philip wasn't keen to take even that small of a sip. How was he to know if Chichester had truly found a spring of fresh water or was merely tapping into the ground water found in this region. He turned his head and took in the faint outline of the tributary that cut through the northern edge of the town where the high street fell away and led out to the salt marshes. It couldn't have been more than a mile away. Surely the spring was too close.

He held on to Grandmother Regina's chair to prevent himself from crossing his arms over his chest in speculation. He was supposed to be supporting Chichester after all.

"I say, is that you, Greylock?"

Philip turned at the sound of Lord Bibury's voice. "Bibury," he returned with a genuine smile. "Has your family coerced you into attending today's festivities?"

Bibury's frown was fierce, but his eyes twinkled with both love and humor. "I'm afraid they have, but I feel a mite better knowing you've been forced to attend as well." He said this with obvious warmth as he bent around Philip to greet Verity and Grandmother.

Philip took the opportunity to scan the walkway leading up to the spring and easily spotted the remainder of the

Lowe family, Ingrid and Winnie flanking their mother as they approached.

By the time Bibury finished telling Grandmother Regina the various improvements he had envisioned for a Bath chair, the rest of the Lowe family had arrived. Winnie went to great and obvious lengths to stand as far away from him as her family would allow. Lady Bibury, however, made it impossible for Winnie to melt away entirely as the countess was drawn to Philip like a dog to a rack of beef.

As it was, there was a rather awkward kerfuffle as Winnie tried to get Ingrid to stand on the other side of her, but Ingrid had her eyes set on standing next to a gentleman Philip supposed was Robert Clarke, who had appeared at her elbow from the crowd like a lovesick fool.

He withdrew the last thought when he realized Ingrid and Robert struck a familiar tableau, one he had engaged in himself only five years ago. His gaze wandered to Winnie who now stood behind her sister, looking entirely at the ground as if this would make her invisible.

His heart tripped at the sight. Had he made things irrevocably worse by telling her he loved her?

He took pity on her and moved to stand on the other side of Aunt Verity. This lasted for all of three seconds until Grandmother Regina complained of a chill, and his aunt suggested they move her to the other side of the statue so as to block the wind. Philip felt no wind, but he didn't wish for his grandmother to fall ill because of his scheming. So he helped Aunt Verity move the chair into the shelter of the statue, thus planting him precisely beside Winnie.

"I'm sorry," he whispered as the buzz of the crowd grew louder around them, and he was fairly sure they wouldn't be overheard.

She ignored him as he thought she would, her head turned entirely to the left at such a severe and resolute angle he was concerned her neck might freeze in such a position. He realized she might think he was apologizing for his actions the previous night when, in fact, he meant their current situation.

"Winnie, I didn't mean—" he tried to clarify, but she stopped him immediately.

"Shhh." She hissed it so loudly two women standing not far in front of them turned casually at the sound, and he bent as if helping Grandmother Regina settle in her chair, and uninterested, the women looked back toward the fountain.

He straightened just as Chichester took a glass from the cart and held it aloft, calling out to the gathered crowd, "Thank you, thank you, thank you all for coming today." He paused, letting the crowd settle.

Philip looked around, taking in the spectators. Quite a sizable group had gathered. He'd been so fixated on waiting for Winnie to arrive that he'd missed it. He had to hand it to Chichester. The man knew how to pull in paying guests.

When he turned back to the fountain where Chichester held court, he saw several young men filling the remaining glasses on the cart with water from the spigot that arched out of the fountain. Water must have been flowing from this particular spring for quite some time if the wear on the rock was any indication, and Philip thought he may be wrong about Chichester tapping into the brackish water.

The young men disseminated the glasses among the guests as Chichester began to speak again. "It is my greatest honor to have you all here today to witness the rebirth of the great Sutton Cross Spring."

This was met with general applause, but Philip kept his hands tucked at his back. It was entirely too early to applaud this man.

"It has been an absolute delight rebuilding this once great

village, and I assure you, we are not finished restoring it to its once former glory. There are many surprises yet to come."

This was met with more cheering, but through the celebratory clapping, Philip heard something else. A grumbling conversation somewhere behind him.

He turned to find two men wearing wool suits patched at the elbows and knees, their boots thick and scuffed with deep creases just past the toe. These men were not dressed like the guests at the hotel, and Philip realized they must be local residents. Local residents who seemed not to agree with Chichester's statement.

Philip turned back around to the festivities at hand, but he kept an ear out to the conversation behind him.

Chichester went on. "It is now time for you all to discover the revitalizing qualities of the Sutton Cross Spring, the very same qualities that until now only I have enjoyed."

Philip waited, and he was rewarded with a snort and a whispered remark from behind him.

"The only one's what enjoyed that water?" Another snort. "Ain't nobody should be enjoying that stuff. Comes straight from the salt marshes, I tell you."

"Does he think no one will notice when the water stops running when the tide goes?" the other man whispered.

Philip didn't hear any more of the conversation. He swung back, his hand seizing Winnie's wrist involuntarily. She instantly tried to pull away from him, but he held fast.

"Winnie, promise me you won't try the water." He leaned dangerously close to her, and if anyone saw them, there would be more than the occasional whisper spread about them. Heads would quite literally turn.

She tugged again at her wrist and leaned into him, her words fierce. "Philip, let go. Someone will see."

"You can't drink the water, Winnie. Please. It will make you sick."

She pulled with greater force now, and he realized the two women who had looked at him before had once more turned about to see what was happening, but he couldn't let go of Winnie's wrist.

"The water is brackish," he pressed on. "If you drink it, you will become ill. Promise me you won't drink it." He realized he was repeating himself, but it was the only way he could think of to get her to listen. It occurred to him that he should be giving the same warning to his grandmother and aunt and the remaining Lowes as well, but he couldn't force himself to move his gaze from Winnie.

He had bent his head to whisper in her ear, but she'd turned her head at his first hushed plea, and they stood there, eye to eye, tensed lips to tensed lips, her wrist still in his hand.

That was when he realized everyone was indeed watching them.

The young men passing out the samples of water had reached them and stopped in confusion at the sight. Philip blinked. Winnie blinked. Yet neither of them broke away.

"Lady Winnaretta?"

Chichester. Damn it.

The marquess had pushed through the first rows of people standing near the fountain and was approaching, his face sharp with concern. For a moment, Philip thought the man truly worried about Winnie, but then he saw the marquess give a quick, scalding look to the men delivering the water and realized he was more concerned for his venture than the woman he planned to marry.

"Lady Winnaretta? What is the problem here?"

Winnie licked her lips. Philip's heart thumped in his chest. This was it. He could keep hold of her wrist and ruin everything for her. Or he could...he could...

"Please help!" he cried, leaning back suddenly but not

releasing Winnie's wrist. "I think the lady is ill!" He widened his eyes suggestively, and Winnie blinked in confusion for only a second.

Right before she fainted dead away.

* * *

"THAT WAS the most romantic thing I have ever witnessed," Ingrid declared as she flounced down on Winnie's bed that afternoon. "I wonder if Robert would ever do anything like that for me." She pursed her lips and looked out the window opposite the bed as if seriously contemplating such a matter.

Winnie snorted. "It was hardly romantic. Chichester tossed me onto a cart headed for the hotel like not much more than a sack of carrots."

Ingrid's gaze swung back to her. "I wasn't speaking of Chichester." She leaned in, her eyes growing bright, her smile eager. "I was speaking of Greylock, of course."

Winnie's insides flashed hot, remembering Philip's grip on her wrist, how her heart had thumped just recalling what had happened in the plunge pool.

But her sister wasn't done, and Winnie allowed herself to be distracted by Ingrid's romantic whimsy. "The way he caught you like that." Ingrid shook her head as if she couldn't quite believe it. "Tell me, sister." Ingrid leaned in again. "Is he terribly strong?"

"Ingrid." Winnie meant her sister's name as a scold, knowing full well the scold was for Winnie herself. As soon as her sister had mentioned it, Winnie was right back there, lying in Philip's strong embrace. It had taken all her strength not to press her palms to his chest, curving over the muscles there. She was supposed to be playing faint after all.

Her sister straightened, her lips flattening to a severe line.

"Oh please, Winnie. It isn't as though you've always been a paragon of virtue. I know you have…urges."

The momentary flash of heat was quickly replaced by the coldness of truth. Ingrid was right. Winnie had had urges, and that was precisely why she was where she was. Sitting in a hotel room bed in Sutton Cross feigning her recovery from a fainting spell.

She swallowed and pushed back the quilts.

There was no point to this, and she certainly wasn't going to waste any more of the day in bed. She had been so certain Chichester would propose while she was here, and she'd spent no more than a few minutes in his company since the moment they had arrived. She knew the man was busy running things for the opening of the hotel, but she had a proposal to secure. It was time to get on with things.

Ingrid scooted off the bed as Winnie gained her feet.

"Is Mother awake from her nap?" Winnie asked, swiftly changing the subject as she reached for her dressing gown. Mother always took a restorative afternoon nap, but Winnie thought it was really just an excuse to hide with the midday papers.

Ingrid crossed her arms over her chest, and Winnie waited to see if her sister would continue her line of prodding, but it seemed even Ingrid knew when it was best to change topics.

"She is," Ingrid finally said. "But I think you'll find her ideas for activities for the remainder of the day rather vexing."

Winnie raised both eyebrows in question.

"She'd like to visit the local printer."

Winnie's eyebrows dropped. "Again? Haven't we visited enough printers?"

Ada Lowe was fond of interrogating small village presses. Winnie released a breath and went to the window Ingrid had been gazing out earlier. From this angle, Winnie could see the rain had returned at some point. Perhaps visiting the local printer wouldn't be so terrible. The list of alternatives was likely shrinking in this weather.

She tugged at her dressing gown belt and turned back to her sister. "I suppose it couldn't get worse, could it?"

Ingrid only smiled. Winnie would recall that smile later when they descended the marble staircase down into the hotel lobby an hour later. At first, she was confused by the quiet that greeted them. Surely everyone had returned from the spring by now. Wouldn't the dining room be serving tea soon? Winnie's stomach chose that moment to growl as if agreeing with her.

She laid a hand on her sister's arm, slowing their progress. From this vantage point, she could take in much of the open space in front of the main doors. The marble floors glistened as though not a single foot had returned from the deluge outside. The seating arrangements were all perfectly squared as though they had remained untouched for some time, and the worst clue of all was the presence of not a single umbrella in the stand by the door.

She looked to her sister, but Ingrid only shrugged. When they rounded the bottom of the stairs, they found their parents nestled into a seating arrangement in the corner. The remains of tea lay scattered on the table in the center of the grouping, and both Mother and Father were lost in the pages of *The Times* and *The Sutton Sentinel*, the press Ada Lowe likely wished to visit that day.

"Good afternoon," Winnie nearly whispered, afraid if she spoke any louder she might startle the entire hotel awake.

Her father set down his newspaper first, the crinkling pages like an explosion in the quiet of the lobby. "Greylock was right, I'm afraid."

Winnie paused, her hands curling around the chair she

had been about to take as she absorbed her father's words. "He was right?" She eased into the chair, hunger moving her forward when apprehension suggested she move carefully.

"The water is brackish," Mother intoned from behind her newsprint.

Ingrid dropped to a chair and began to peck at the tea remains. "What does brackish mean?"

Winnie grabbed a watercress sandwich and nearly shoved the thing into her mouth. Brackish? Oh no. What would this mean for Chichester? Would he not propose now? Lud, she was terrible thinking of such a thing right then.

"The water in the supposed spring is not from a spring. Chichester must have tapped into the water table and found a source connected to the salt marshes." Her father pinned her with a gaze so heavy, Winnie reached for another sandwich.

She knew perfectly well what her father thought of her plan to marry Chichester, but she held her chin firm. He couldn't possibly know all of her reasons for it, and she wouldn't let him break her with his penetrating gaze alone.

"The water contains enough salt to cause stomach upset."

Winnie and Ingrid both looked at their mother whose eyes remained on the inches of ink in her hands.

"Stomach upset?" Ingrid asked, but Winnie had already figured it out, her eyes traveling round the empty lobby once more.

"The guests are all ill," Winnie whispered, her fingers curling into her skirts. This couldn't be happening. Chichester had said her time here would be life changing. How life changing could it be if he were preoccupied with a hotel full of sick guests?

"Very."

Winnie turned back to her father to find his gaze had not

relented in the slightest. She felt the urge to swallow but resisted.

"We're fortunate your fainting spell brought us back to the hotel before we too could succumb," her father went on. "Strange, how you've never fainted before in your life."

Winnie reached for a lemon tart this time, stuffing the whole thing into her mouth so she needn't reply.

Finally Mother looked away from her newspaper. "And the Hodges, of course. It was so kind of Philip and his aunt to help us return. It's lucky they did or they too would be ill."

Winnie pressed a hand to her chest, pushing against the sudden pain there.

Philip.

First the fan for Ingrid and now this. He'd saved her and her family from illness. Yet…

He hadn't called out Chichester for it. In her mind, she could see the events of that morning play out like a terrible storybook. Philip's grip on her wrist, Chichester surging through the crowd, demanding to know what was amiss. Philip could have said right then what he'd suspected.

But he didn't.

In that moment, he'd looked at her, and in his eyes, she saw…she saw…

She saw everything.

She swallowed and reached for the teapot only to find her sister had poured a cup for her. Drinking it all in one gulp, it gave her no relief. Her heart still pounded, her stomach twisted in knots, and her mind remained a cloudy mess.

Philip.

She needed air. Her eyes went to the bank of windows along the one wall and found them spotted with rain. She'd get her cloak then and boots. She would be fine. She just must—

"Greylock!"

Winnie froze, her hands on the arms of the chair as she had meant to push herself to her feet, but her father's exclamation had her body seizing.

"Bibury." Philip's voice was just as warm in greeting, and her heart raced.

She wanted to look at him but couldn't summon the courage.

Her father stood. "I'd like to thank you again, young man, for your astute observation at the spring." He gestured around them at the silence. "As you can see the waters have taken their toll."

Finally Winnie allowed herself a peek in Philip's direction and saw to her surprise he was dressed for the outdoors with boots, greatcoat, and hat.

"I'm only glad I intervened in time," Philip said modestly.

Mother turned in her chair, her smile wide. "And I wish to thank you for your assistance with Winnie, my lord. It is much appreciated."

Did her mother just wink at Philip?

Winnie frowned ferociously in her mother's direction, but her mother was oblivious, her smile focused on Philip. Winnie might as well not even be present.

She finally pushed to her feet. "If you will excuse me, I think I am in need of some fresh air," she said, pressing a hand to her forehead. "I've been in my room for so long, you see."

Her mother never even glanced in her direction as she made her excuses, but she could feel her father's stare on her back as she made her way to the staircase.

She was so focused on her escape she didn't notice when the front doors opened, emitting a gust of damp air and a pair of guests speckled with rain and loaded with servants and trunks and valises.

Winnie stopped to give them room to enter the hotel and

escape the rain, but her legs vibrated, wishing to keep moving forward, get her cloak and boots, and escape herself.

There was a great deal of confusion as it seemed the lobby was understaffed that afternoon. A woman in a starched uniform who appeared to be in charge made excuses for the lack of staff, citing an incident that required a great deal of attention. Winnie could only imagine what was hidden in the word *incident*, and her eyes drifted up, thinking of all the poor guests who had taken ill and what was now required of the staff to care for them.

She let her gaze linger around the hotel, noting the obvious absence of Chichester, but then, he had drunk from the spring himself, hadn't he? Oh dear. She hadn't thought of that. What if he were too ill to propose?

Her future hadn't seemed quite so heavy until that moment. She thought of her father's stare only minutes earlier and wondered not for the first time if she had chosen the right course of action. But then, she really had no choice, did she?

It seemed they had finally cleared up the confusion of the trunks, and a maid stepped forward to take the outer things of the guests, unwrapping them from the many layers they had obviously donned before heading out into the weather.

Winnie found herself smiling politely as she knew soon she would need to step around the guests and finish making her way to the stairs, only the smile soon froze into place, her muscles unable to move. One of the guests had pushed back the hood of her cloak, exposing hair the color of burnished bronze, a color so peculiar, so rare, it could only be one person.

"Genevieve." She breathed the name before she realized what she was doing, and the head turned sharply as if in surprise.

And then there she was. Genevieve.

Winnie couldn't make her mind form the proper sounds, an introduction, a greeting—

An apology.

Mathilda's words came back to Winnie in a flash, and her stomach heaved, wondering not for the first time how much of what she remembered from that time had been the truth and how much she had fabricated to keep herself safe when she hurt so very much.

She stood there, suspended in the moment, realizing only too late that she was waiting for Genevieve's reaction. Somehow the woman's response in that moment would tell Winnie everything. Would tell Winnie if she had been wrong all this time. If she had been wrong in thinking her friend had abandoned her, in not realizing just how much she had pushed people away during those dark days.

Winnie knew the moment Genevieve spotted her. It was the exact moment her face split into a grin, a grin that spoke of years of shared delight, of childish antics, of adventure and…fun.

"Winnie." Genevieve spoke her name with the breathlessness of excitement and surprise, and Winnie's heart broke at the hope she heard in the woman's voice.

Had Mathilda been right? Had Winnie pushed everyone away? Even her very best friend?

"Genevieve, I—" She'd never know if she had meant to apologize, if she had meant to make amends, because at that moment Genevieve slipped her cloak from her shoulders, and Winnie saw the rest of her once best friend.

Genevieve was very much pregnant.

Run.

The word screamed through her mind, her brain attempting to protect her, to save her from the hurt that began to radiate through her body in unrelenting waves of torment.

Run.

She couldn't breathe. The walls were so much closer, the floor sweeping up toward her, threatening to topple her right over. She couldn't *breathe.*

Run.

Like a tidal wave, she couldn't stop it. The compulsion to flee. She had to get away from the thing that hurt her even as her friend's face registered her mistake, as her eyes widened in sympathy as her mouth trembled with words of regret. It didn't matter.

Winnie was already running, through the doors and out into the rain as if the storm could finally rid her of her sorrows.

CHAPTER 11

*I*t was like watching a terrible carriage collision and being unable to stop it.

Philip had settled Aunt Verity and Grandmother in their rooms with a luncheon tray and orders to the maid to bring tea, lots of it. He had been worried his grandmother would suffer ill effects from all the excitement, but the woman only clapped her hands with glee and told any maid who would listen about the big to do at the fountain.

It had taken him far longer than he wished to extricate himself. He left their rooms with the determination to set things right between he and Winnie after what had happened in the plunge pool. It was only luck that he had found the Lowes in the lobby because he wouldn't have stopped himself from knocking on her door if he must.

She may have said she loved Chichester, she may have said she intended to marry him, she may have said she was trying to help Ingrid, but her actions told an entirely different story. One he intended to uncover that day. They would conduct a calm and polite conversation in the open for all to see if only to keep their obvious attraction at bay long enough to reach an understanding.

The events of that morning had proven just how precarious this game was they were playing. He wouldn't have cared at all if his actions didn't directly affect Ingrid. She was an innocent in all of this, and he didn't wish for his interactions with Winnie to cause her harm or affect her future prospects. It was past time to set things straight.

He had excused himself from the Lowes as quickly as possible after Winnie had made her exit, thinking a walk outside would be the perfect opportunity to speak to her without anyone else overhearing them and causing further problems but keeping them safely within the public eye.

He retraced his steps to the staircase, thinking she may have gone up to her rooms to fetch a cloak or hat. The weather was proving to be rather unforgivable, but the rain was light, and a small walk wouldn't do much harm. Only Winnie hadn't gone upstairs.

He found her standing perfectly still, her arms stiff at her sides, her fingers spread wide as if frozen in shock, but he only saw her for a second. Because then his eyes riveted to the person standing just inside the doors. He recognized Genevieve even five years later. It was hard not to with her unusually colored hair. She looked much as she had when he'd last seen her. She had pale skin and wide blue eyes that only emphasized her smile.

Standing behind her was a gentleman Philip didn't recognize, but as he reached for Genevieve's cloak, he thought him her husband. But then the gentleman took the cloak, and Philip's stomach lurched.

Genevieve was with child.

No.

He thought he might be sick right there in the lobby of the

Hotel Sutton Cross. His stomach heaved into his throat at the same time his heart beat a staccato. His hands reached forward before he could stop himself, as if he could grab hold of Winnie and keep her from falling apart through his touch alone.

But she was already moving, running, going through the doors and into the rain, leaving Genevieve standing in the lobby, the rain dripping from the hem of her skirts, those wide eyes lost and confused.

He didn't bother to stop and explain to her. He only ran after Winnie, the need to find her, to touch her, to keep her from shattering the single thought pushing through him.

He was met with a wall of wind as soon as he stepped free of the main doors. The long line of carriages that had waited there only the day before was gone and a single footman hovered in the shelter of the scaffolding he had sought refuge in himself.

Winnie.

He turned in the only direction he thought she might go, retracing her steps up to the high street where the disastrous interlude at the fountainhead had taken place. He spotted her with ease as the street was empty at that hour, the rain keeping others indoors. The wind buffeted her, swiping at her skirts and tossing her hair. She stumbled, her slippered feet sliding on the now trampled boards that had made up the walkway, their surfaces slick with moisture.

He caught up to her in seconds, his own booted feet surer through the mess. While the wind was menacing, the rain, he discovered, was not as terrible as he had feared it would be. It spitted more than fell, and it was like slogging through the last spurts of a once great deluge. Still he was coated in the fine mist before he reached her, and he knew she couldn't stay out in this, not without a proper coat or footwear.

He shucked his own greatcoat as he approached her, slowing his steps so as not to startle her. Still, her head swung round as he laid the greatcoat across her shoulders. Even though the need to touch her had been so great just minutes before, he couldn't touch her now. Not now that he saw how rigid her shoulders were, how carefully she pressed her hands to her stomach, how wide and frightened her eyes were.

He only laid his coat across her shoulders and stepped back, matching her pace at a measured distance. She snuck only one more glance in his direction as if to assure herself that he wouldn't try to stop her, and then she kept on.

And kept on and on.

They swiftly reached the high street, but instead of turning left toward the fountainhead as he'd expected her to do, she turned right, heading down the high street toward the end of town to the lane that led out to the salt marshes. Sutton Cross was perched on a small elevation before the land fell away and down to the Great Ouse, which traveled all the way to the channel. He'd never traveled to this part of Norfolk, but he pictured the coastline in his mind, if only to think of what trouble Winnie may inadvertently stumble across.

He could tell within minutes that she wasn't truly seeing where she was going. Her eyes didn't change, and she didn't move her head about as though she were scanning her course. She simply moved, her legs swishing now as her skirts became soaked with rain that ran off the end of the greatcoat.

He looked back the way they had come, but they had traveled so far now Sutton Cross was only a dim shape on the horizon. He turned and took in the skyline, watching the thick gray clouds roil toward them.

They had nearly reached the salt marshes when he finally dared to touch her.

She jumped, her eyes wild when she turned to him.

He pointed to the sky, at the threatening clouds. "We can't stay out here, Winnie. We must find shelter. Let me take you back to the—"

"No." The single word tore through the wind and left no room for argument.

Not that he would have tried. She was already walking away from him, and he ran to catch up to her.

They walked on, the clouds growing thicker, the sky darkening with every step. They were too far from the village now, and he kept his gaze scanning the salt marshes, looking for anything that might serve as a shelter. They had passed several stone ruins that looked to be Roman, and he wondered if there had been a fortification here once. Perhaps there was a larger structure somewhere in which they could take cover if the storm should break upon them.

But even as he searched, he could see nothing.

Winnie turned off the main lane then, so suddenly he had almost walked past her before he realized she'd turned. He scrambled to catch her, afraid to let her stray too far. Salt marshes could be deadly if one stepped in the wrong place, one's feet soon swallowed by sand and mud. The wind was stronger here along the shore, and he held his hands in front of him, ready to catch Winnie should she tumble.

But it was like there was no wind at all. Her stride never wavered, her gaze never wandering.

He could feel her pain as if it were his own, and he hated more than anything that he could do nothing for it.

He spotted the stone house at the edge of the salt marsh at the moment the sky opened, and the rain fell in a thick cascade, drenching them within moments.

He seized Winnie's shoulders and wouldn't let go, no matter her protests. "We'll die if we stay out here," he shouted over the roar of the storm.

He felt her shoulders go loose at his words, and he knew

she understood. He pulled her in the direction he had spotted the roof, hoping it sat atop enough of a structure to give them shelter. He pushed through the reeds, keeping his eyes on his feet to ensure he stood on solid ground. Finally, after what seemed ages, his foot struck hard ground, and he realized they'd circled back around to land. He looked up, and relief washed through him.

He'd been wrong. It wasn't a stone house. It was a dovecote, a small building nestled into the scrubby trees and brush along this side of the salt marsh. It was old and bore two Christian crosses carved into the worn stone on one side with a single mullioned window between them. Definitely Roman, he decided, but it didn't matter. It was completely solid, all four walls still standing, and he surged toward it.

The door was comprised of iron and wood, and someone had wedged a length of metal through the old padlock ring to keep the door secure. He pried it free, letting go of Winnie just long enough to get the door open, and then he hurtled them both inside.

The sudden silence rang in his ears as he took in the space around them. He blinked and wiped the rain from his eyes as he tried to understand where they were. The building had looked like a converted dovecote from the outside, but he thought someone might be using it for other purposes now. A small cot was pushed to one side. It was bare of quilts, but the mattress was thick and unstained. The floor was dry, remarkably so, and a small stove sat in one corner with a pile of kindling stacked beside it. The only other furniture was a narrow table and a chair that had been repaired more than once.

He went to the stove, sending up a silent prayer that the chimney wasn't clogged. They would need heat if they weren't to catch cold or worse. He piled some kindling into the stove, stripping the wood bare of its bark until he'd made a small nest into which he struck the flint he found on top of the stove. Sparks showered the shredded bark until finally a flame caught.

He sat back, kneeling on the dirt floor, willing the fire to catch. He could feel Winnie somewhere behind him, but he couldn't bring himself to look at her. His heart hurt so much then, sitting there on the dirt floor, the past welling up around them as if it might suffocate them.

It was Winnie who spoke first.

"I'm sorry." He hadn't been expecting an apology and swung about at this, his rebuttal on his lips, but she continued. "I always think I'm all right. That I've accepted…what happened, but then I see—" Her voice broke, the sound wet with unshed tears and filled with fathomless sorrow.

He was already on his feet, his arms going round her, tucking her head under his chin. They stood like that, held together by a grief they'd never before been able to share. It struck him then, the injustice of it. Of Winnie suffering through everything she had without him, and suddenly he was angry. Angry that he couldn't have been there *with* her.

Because suddenly it didn't matter, this struggle that had sprung up between them after so much time apart, the sides so clearly marked. There shouldn't have been any sides. It should have always been them, together, facing this terrible thing, the loss of the baby they had each imagined separately, the loss of the future they had started to build together.

"Winnie." He said her name because he had nothing else to say. His heart beat too furiously, his blood pounded too angrily at all the time that was lost.

How many other times had she suffered like this? How many other times had she been alone in her grief when she should have been sharing it with him?

He wasn't sure who pulled back first but instead of holding her, he was looking into her eyes, finding there the same conclusion he had just reached. He saw the heartache, the longing, and the regret, but most importantly, he saw understanding, disbelief at what was before her. It wasn't her; it wasn't him. It was *them.*

Distantly he heard the storm rage around them, the growling wind and beating rain, and the stone building shuddered but held fast as it had for likely hundreds of years. And in the middle of it, they stood, arms wrapped around each other, holding on just as the stones surrounding them held on. And when their lips finally met, he knew he would never again let go.

* * *

IT WAS LIKE MAGIC.

She wanted to laugh at her own absurdness, at her own terribly cliched thoughts. But that was what went through her mind when Philip kissed her.

Magic.

Because when Philip kissed her the rest vanished.

The panic that had seized her chest, that had propelled her legs forward through the rain, across the salt marsh to—wherever the hell they were now, it disappeared the moment his lips touched hers.

It wasn't about desire or attraction or greed. It was something more complicated than that, almost something magical within itself. His touch had the power to dispel the things that plagued her, that ground their way into her very soul and were kept painfully suspended somewhere between panic and worry.

But it was all gone now, gone but not forgotten as she could feel the all-consuming grief hovering just out of her reach. It was like a shadow that chased her, but no matter how fast she ran it always caught up to her. She couldn't keep running. She knew that. She was just so very tired, and one day when the need to run came, she knew she wouldn't have the strength to answer its call.

But now, with Philip all around her, she wondered if she wouldn't need to. If maybe, the next time the pain came, she could lean on him instead and find, if not relief, peace.

Peace.

Her heart screamed for the word. The idea that this pain that haunted her might not be so much to bear. But of course it wouldn't. It wouldn't be so much if she weren't so alone.

A hiccup of despair lodged in her throat, and she turned away from the sudden image of her future married to the Marquess of Chichester. The man was a liar, a cheat, and a fraud. No matter what she'd tried to convince Philip of, no matter what she'd tried to convince herself of, she *knew* that. She knew what her future would entail, and it wouldn't be this.

This.

Oh God, this.

The way Philip cupped her face with his hands, so gently, so preciously, the way his lips skated over hers, comforting, pleasing, giving instead of taking. He always gave her so much. Her heart constricted, the pain almost too much to bear.

No.

The word whispered through her mind. No, not now. Don't think of it. Think of only him. Philip. Just Philip. Them, together. There was no grief, there was no loss, there was no pain. It was just them, and the magic that simmered around them like an aura.

The cold drop of water on her forehead had her rearing back, her eyes flying upward as if expecting the ceiling of their unexpected shelter to cave in, but it wasn't that. Philip hadn't removed his hat, and water dripped from the brim of it, droplets cascading on her as they'd kissed.

She laughed, the sound soft and unsure in the stillness. Philip looked up as if realizing for the first time that he still wore his hat, and the silly expression on his face made her laugh again.

It felt light and easy, laughing with him like that, and suddenly the past five years were erased. All of it was erased. Nothing terrible had ever happened. It was just them, and this unexpected thing that existed between them.

Love. That was what Philip had said standing in the plunge pool, and it had taken everything she had not to tell him she loved him too.

Her insides were a mess now, her heart pounding, her stomach twisting itself into knots, cold and hot running through her at once. But then Philip reached up and grasped the brim of his hat, tossing it aside like he hadn't a care in the world.

She laughed again and without thinking, reached up and shoved his greatcoat from her shoulders. She was still soaked and so was he, but somehow this was terribly funny.

It seemed impossible that she should be smiling then, but the rest of the world was so far away just then. Perhaps it was the feeling of being wrapped snuggly in a cocoon thanks to the roar of the storm outside. Perhaps it was just being there with him.

She became aware of a warmth somewhere beside them and realized the wood in the stove had caught now, a small fire burning eagerly. Her smile changed then, her hands moving without her knowledge.

"We should get out of these wet things, shouldn't we? We might catch a chill." She found the tie under her breasts that kept her bodice cinched. Her fingers were cold and clumsy, but she managed to loosen the knot. She made to shrug it off her shoulders, but she looked up then and caught Philip watching her, and the look in his eyes stole her breath.

He came forward then, his hands closing over hers. He studied her eyes for an intense moment before saying, "Winnie, you don't need to do this. I don't want—" He licked his lips, and she realized he was nervous. It seemed so odd to see him like that, and it went straight to her heart. Philip. Philip who was always making things better should be so uncertain now. "I don't want you to do this because you're hurting or because you think I—"

She pulled one hand free to lay her fingers on his lips, stilling his words. She made sure he was listening before she said, "I'm doing this because I want you, Philip." She watched his eyes change, darken. "I've always wanted you." She nearly whispered the words, not quite believing she was saying them, finally, after all this time.

This time when he kissed her it was with a hard edge of hunger that sent a thrill through her, banishing the chill of the rain and the cold of grief. Philip was more alive to her than ever, and her body sang in response.

She arched into him, heedless of the wet clothes that still separated them. But it didn't last. Soon his hands took over where hers had started, and her gown crumpled in a wet heap to the floor. She shoved his coat from his shoulders, her fingers working loose the buttons of his waistcoat before starting on his cravat. The air was filled with the sound of wet clothes being carelessly discarded, but she noticed none of it as her hands finally found his warm skin again, and sheer pleasure rocketed through her.

"Philip," she breathed against his neck. "Oh God, Philip."

Their movements became a blur then as they tried to remove the rest of their clothing, each tearing at the other. It was as though there was an unspoken agreement between them, each needing to feel the other, skin to skin, in some basic need for connection.

But then Philip pulled away far too soon, and he left her standing there in her chemise, stockings, and ruined slippers. He retrieved his greatcoat from the floor and spread it over the mattress of the cot. He was still turning when she stepped into his arms, but he held her back.

"Winnie, I…" His voice died away as he searched her face, and she hated the uncertainty she saw there, knowing it was her fault.

She kissed him. She kissed him with all she had, hoping he could understand the things she couldn't say.

When his arms came around her this time, she gave herself over to him, completely, if only for this one time.

For what did it matter?

She'd already lost so much, and she would lose even more still when she married Chichester. She could have this one time. Just this once with Philip.

A shiver spread through her when her back touched the chilled greatcoat, and she jerked against Philip. His eyes widened in concern, his arms wrapping more tightly around her.

She smiled reassuringly. "You'll need to warm me," she whispered.

The look on his face then was anything but uncertain. He backed away but only long enough to shed the rest of his clothes and help her with her chemise, peeling away her ruined shoes and stockings. There was nothing sensual about it. Their movements were desperate, needy, and urgent.

They had waited five years for this.

The thought struck her then even as he pulled the chemise over her head. She had thought it was only her who had fallen so long ago. He had never needed to say the words. But she knew now that Philip had too. It was in the way he traced kisses along her jaw, down her neck, along her collar-bone as if he were marking his territory, afraid that it might slip from his grasp again.

Her stomach tightened, and for a moment, the guilt threatened to consume her. Because she would leave him again. She must.

His hands reached her aching breasts, and she arched, giving herself to him. He took, and suddenly she no longer felt the cold. He'd banished it from her with the simple touch of his lips, the stroke of a hand. God, he was everywhere, and yet she couldn't get enough of him.

She ran her hands up his back, memorizing each curve of muscle, each indent of bone. This was what she'd almost had five years ago. While her heart had fallen, she hadn't allowed herself more, and now she almost regretted it. Would they have had more time? Could she have had this more than once?

She felt the tears sting her eyes and pushed the thoughts away. She had now, and that had to be enough.

His lips had made their way to her stomach, to the curve of her hip, lower until she couldn't reach him anymore.

"Philip," she moaned, hating the loss of him.

But then he scraped his teeth along her hip bone, and she collapsed back against the mattress, desire shooting through her with an intensity that stole her breath.

He was back suddenly, capturing her mouth in a kiss that devastated her. He cradled her, picking her up off the mattress in his arms as he settled between her legs. She opened for him, and she felt him, his hard length pressing against the softness of her belly. Suddenly a desire so strong surged through her, and she lifted her hips, needing to feel him inside of her.

"Please," she breathed against his neck. She ran her hands

over his shoulders and up his neck until her fingers plunged into his hair.

God, had she remembered how strong he was? How broad his shoulders? But of course they had been little more than children then, so young and naive. She had thought he would save her from all the terrible things in the world, but she hadn't known then that the terrible thing was her.

She kissed him, holding on to him with everything she had as his hands skated down her body, leaving a trail of fire until he cupped her buttocks, lifting her until he was at her entrance. She could feel him, hard and pulsing, and she whimpered, suddenly wanting nothing more than to have him inside of her.

"Please, Philip," she said against his lips, her hands cupping his face. "Please. I need you inside of me." She was all but begging now, and she could feel his smile against her mouth.

She didn't care. The tension that had been building inside of her for so long, longer than she could have imagined, grew to unbearable heights, and she needed him, his touch, his kiss, his everything.

Still he held back, his hand wandering over her hip, tracing the delicate skin at the inside of her thigh, moving slowly until finally—*finally*—he touched her. Just a single blunt finger against her most sensitive nub. She jerked, her heart thumping in her chest, as her eyes flew open to find him watching her with a look so sincere and complete it shook her.

She couldn't look away as his finger began to move against her, as the tension spun inside of her, as she raised her hips, wanting more. He kept his finger against her nub as he pushed at her entrance, just a little and then a little more, teasing her with every shift but never giving her what she wanted.

"Please." She was nearly crying now, the tension unbearable.

When he thrust inside of her, completely and deeply, she nearly came.

"Oh God, Winnie," he said, his forehead pressed against hers. "I can't...I can't..." He sucked in a breath as she lifted her hips, bringing him deeper.

She kissed him, wrapping her arms around him and holding him tightly to her. He thrust again, his finger circling her nub, and she wanted so much to hold that moment forever, but it was too much. When she came, it was with an intensity she'd never known and knew she'd never know again. Her heart would have broken right then if he weren't holding her so tightly when his own release came, and for a moment, she forgot this wasn't forever and let herself be carried away.

$\mathcal{H}$e would have lain there forever if the chill hadn't overcome him.

The small stove was doing a fine job of emitting heat, but it wasn't enough when they'd been soaked through from the storm. He roused himself long enough to stand and fetch his shirt, which was relatively dry considering, and gave it to Winnie while he tended to the fire.

The stack of kindling was generous, and he wasn't worried they would run out. His only concern was in how long the storm would continue before they could try to make their way back to the village. He doubted anyone would notice their disappearance as the majority of the guests were all sick in their beds, but he didn't wish for her family to worry about her.

The way she'd run out the door into the rain had been gut-wrenching. He was certain her family was concerned, and he didn't wish to prolong their worrying, even though every part of him wanted to remain secluded in the dovecote forever. It was rather cozy, and he understood why someone had made a kind of refuge here. He would need to replace the kindling or at least leave some coins for the trouble.

With the fire roaring now, he crept back into bed, his feet icy from the dirt floor. Winnie hadn't spoken in the few minutes he'd left the bed, and he pulled her into his arms now, cradling her against him as he wrapped the end of the greatcoat around them both. It wasn't much, but it would do to keep them warm for now.

The sound of the rain still tapped against the roof, and he could feel himself drifting, but he wished to reassure Winnie first. He smoothed back her hair, noticing it had almost dried.

"You mustn't worry," he said. "I'll speak to your father as soon as we return to the village."

She reared up so quickly it nearly knocked him from the bed. Her eyes were wild, her nearly dried hair sticking up in all directions from her head. "You'll do what?"

"Speak to your father," he said more clearly now. "I thought you might be worried that…"

He let his voice trail off as she scrambled over him to get off the cot. He watched her, apprehension pooling in his stomach. She collected her dress and chemise as though she meant to put them both on at the same time, but she was still wearing his shirt, and her garments were still soaked. She wrestled with the wet fabric for several seconds before giving up.

He sat up. "Winnie, what is the matter?"

He wasn't sure why he asked. A part of him already knew what was happening.

"I need to get back, Philip. I can't be found here."

She didn't mean in the dovecote. She meant she couldn't be found with him. Because if she were found with him…

"What are you talking about? You know I'll marry you. You mustn't worry—"

She dropped the gown and chemise, her eyes going directly to his. "Philip, I can't marry you. I'm intended for the Marquess of Chichester. You know that."

There it was, his fears spoken plainly as if there was nothing more over which to argue.

He stood, wrapping himself in his greatcoat. This was not a conversation he wished to have naked. He grabbed her shoulders, if only to stop her frenzied, useless movements with her gown and chemise. "No, Winnie, I don't know. You've never explained it to me."

Her movements ceased as though he'd struck a nerve, and this time when she met his gaze, the manic look he'd seen there earlier had dissolved into something like regret. It was like a dagger directly to his heart. He had been so sure he wasn't alone in his feelings, not then and not now, but seeing her face in that moment, he wasn't so sure.

He released her, suddenly no longer wishing to even touch her. He paced as far away as the small dovecote would let him as he said, "And you're not going to explain it to me, are you?" He turned only his head to find her standing where he'd left her, the sodden gown and chemise still in her hands.

Her mouth opened, no words coming forth as her eyes seemed to plead with him. "I can't, Philip…"

He didn't know if she was saying she couldn't explain or she couldn't marry him. He didn't like either of those options.

Turning away, he picked up his trousers, waistcoat, and cravat from the floor. He took extraordinary and painful care in laying out his things upon the narrow table and mended chair, hoping they might dry in the heat from the stove. Even when he'd finished he stood there for several more seconds, drawing careful breaths to calm himself.

How was it just minutes ago he thought all of his desires had come true? And now he felt as though the entire world were falling down around his shoulders, and his heart was shattering again like it had five years ago.

When he thought he had better control of himself, he turned back around to find Winnie trying to get her chemise over her head. He stepped forward, pulling the garment from between her hands.

She looked up, her mouth set, her nostrils flaring, and he held up a hand.

"Listen." He didn't say anything more, and her eyes narrowed. Her body radiated as if ready for a fight, and he felt the loss of the closeness of minutes before all over again. It was like a wave of sadness rolling through him, wiping out any hope in its path.

She raised her eyebrows as if in question when he didn't speak, and he simply raised a hand, pointing to the roof where the sound of rain was like a herd of stampeding tiny feet. Without a response, she yanked her chemise out of his grip.

"We can't go out in this," he finally said. "We must wait for the rain to let up."

"I can't wait," she said, the words muffled as she faced away from him again.

She shucked his shirt then, and for a moment, the soft light from the stove danced along the curve of her spine. He was forced to look away, unable to bear the sight of all that skin. Desire still flared in him, and he hated himself for his weakness.

He heard more rustling and the tear of fabric, but he didn't turn back around until he heard her attempting to put her ruined slippers back on. Only then did he say, "Winnie, I must insist you stay here. It's not safe."

She spun around at the same time he turned to face her, and they nearly collided in the small space. "You don't understand, Philip. I cannot be found here. It would ruin everything."

"Then tell me, Winnie. Tell me why it would ruin everything because I don't understand. I—" He'd almost said he loved her again, but the words stopped, stuck against the back of his teeth. He was in so much pain. He couldn't tell her that again; he couldn't give her another way to hurt him.

"I must marry Chichester. You know that."

He paced away from her, feeling the blood in his veins heat every time she repeated herself. He spiked his fingers through his hair and closed his eyes. It was useless. He would get nowhere with this line of questioning. When he opened his eyes, he began to dress, fighting into each piece of sodden clothing. When he was finally dressed, he found his hat where it had toppled to the dirt floor and brushed it off before sticking it back on his head.

He glanced at Winnie as he went for the door. It must have swelled with the rain, and it stuck as he tried to open it. He was met with a sheet of rain as he had thought he would and wished once more that he could make Winnie find reason. This was a foolish idea to try to return to the hotel now. But she was already standing behind him. She'd tried to tame her hair into some kind of twist, but it only accentuated the wildness of her expression.

There was nothing to be done for it. He stepped out into the rain.

He was soaked instantly, but he hardly noticed it. Holding out his arm for her, he helped Winnie from the dovecote before securing the door behind them. The spongy ground of the salt marsh had turned to mud, and walking proved treacherous, but Winnie was already several paces in front of him before he'd finished with the door.

It wasn't until they'd almost reached the salt marsh proper

that he realized their mistake. The rain made it nearly impossible to see, especially as the wind whipped it into his face, and he held a hand in front of his eyes to keep going, one painful step at a time. Reeds tangled about his legs, impeding him further, as he struggled on, and he was concentrating so much on his steps that he didn't look up until it was almost too late.

The tide had come in. The salt marsh was perilously flooded, but in the rain, it was almost entirely camouflaged. The rippling water before them where the salt marsh had once been might have just been a trick of the frenzied rain, but it wasn't. They were cut off.

But Winnie wasn't looking up. She too was carefully watching her feet and—

He seized her elbow just in time and yanked her back. She tumbled, falling against his chest.

"Philip! You must—" She shouted over the roar of the wind.

He pressed his lips almost to her ear so she could hear him. "The tide's come in. We can't cross the salt marsh. It's too dangerous."

Her head whipped around before he finished, and he was forced to jerk his head back to keep from being clipped. He knew the moment she realized what had happened. The muscles under his hand tightened at the same time she stopped pulling against his grip.

She shook her head. "No." He felt the word more than heard it.

He tugged on her arm. "We need to go back to the dovecote. We can try again in the morning." She resisted as he knew she would, but he held fast. "Winnie, don't do this. You can't marry Chichester if you drown." He hated saying the words, but just then, it seemed the only way to get her attention.

It worked. She went slack, falling against him as her feet slipped in the mud.

They retraced their steps back to the dovecote. It was worse than when they had managed it not minutes before, and he knew they would need to wait until morning now. He wasn't sure how long they had been walking before the storm had set upon them, but he knew now it must be late evening, although the sky was black with clouds, making it impossible to tell. If the tide were in now, they would need to head out at first light to cross the marsh while the tide was still low enough.

This time when he got the door to the dovecote pried open they swept in a puddle of water with them. He got it shut as quickly as possible behind them, but the floor by the door had turned to mud. He helped Winnie past it before shedding his coat and hat. He left the rest of his clothes on this time, and after tending the fire again, he pulled out the chair by the table while Winnie sat uncomfortably on the cot.

Neither of them spoke, but it didn't matter. He needed to think, think about how he could convince Winnie to see to reason, and it appeared as if he would have all night to do so.

* * *

SHE DIDN'T KNOW when she started shivering. The only reason she realized she was even doing it was because she heard a funny rustling noise and discovered it was her hands against the folds of her skirts. She looked down, staring at her hands as though she'd never seen them before. It was only then that the cold hit her. She sucked in a breath, her teeth crashing against each other as the shivering took hold in earnest.

"Philip." She didn't know why she said his name. It was

only that she couldn't move her mind beyond the shaking that now gripped her.

They had been sitting in silence for some time, and it was her fault really. It wasn't until Philip had wrestled the door shut on the dovecote that she understood what had happened.

She had failed.

It was no longer about one night with the man she loved. By not being able to return before they were discovered missing, she had most assuredly destroyed her reputation. Chichester would never marry her now. He couldn't. If he wished to continue his rise in society through his investments, he needed a wife above reproach, one who would elevate his standing, not drag it down.

She had ruined everything and all because of her weakness of character. If only she hadn't run away. If only she could be stronger. What was wrong with her? She'd lost the baby five years ago. She should be fine now. Why did she have to be like this?

Hands were on her, and she realized Philip had stood and was trying to strip her of her gown.

"You must help me," he said then. "You need to get out of this."

There was nothing anticipatory now about how he removed her clothes. How he wrapped her in his coat and made her lie down on the cot he had dragged closer to the fire. She lay there, huddled in the coat that smelled like him, like them. Had it only happened hours before? How could everything have fallen apart so quickly?

She stared at the flames flickering behind the grate of the stove, vaguely aware that Philip was trying to spread out her gown and chemise so they would dry. She didn't even know she was speaking until Philip appeared in her vision again, concern written on his face.

He sat on the cot bedside her, one hand gentle on her shoulder. "Winnie, what is it? Are you in pain? Are you ill?"

She shook her head against the mattress, her hair crackling. "Ingrid won't marry Robert now. I've ruined everything."

"Why can't Ingrid marry Robert? You've done such a fine job presenting her. Surely the Clarkes will approve of the match."

She blinked. "No, they won't. Not unless I marry Chichester, and he won't marry me now. I'm ruined."

Philip's hand stilled on her shoulder, and something inside of her opened. So she'd finally told him. There was nothing left to keep from him. It didn't matter if he tried to stop the engagement. There would be no engagement now.

"What are you saying, Winnie? Was someone forcing you to marry Chichester?" His voice was so kind it brought tears to her eyes, but they didn't fall. She held them in like she held everything in.

"I must marry him so the Clarkes will think I'm worthy. That I'm not beyond redemption. That Ingrid is not ruined by association."

The cot shifted, and Philip appeared in front of her. He must be kneeling on the floor. He touched her face.

"You're not beyond redemption, Winnie. Why would you think that?"

She closed her eyes, unable to look at him when she said it. "Because I fell in love with you when I was carrying my dead lover's baby." She hiccupped, the tears forcing their way through her defenses. "Because I run away from pregnant women."

She didn't hear him move but suddenly he was lying next to her, holding her against him, body to body as she cried. She cried for Julia. She cried for William. She cried for Philip. And she even let herself cry for herself. Through it all

Philip only held her. He didn't try to stop her; he didn't try to comfort her with meaningless words. He just held her.

After what seemed an eternity, she ran out of tears, and she lay there, spent in his arms as the rain drummed against the roof, wrapping them in the obscurity of the sound.

Philip touched her hair, smoothing it from her face as he said, "You're not disgraced, Winnie, and you're not somehow broken because you run away from pregnant women."

She met his gaze, tilting only her head to do so, not wanting to leave the shelter of his arms. "How can you say that?"

"Because running away doesn't mean you're broken. It means you haven't allowed yourself to grieve."

"Grieve? But William—"

"I'm not speaking of William." He said nothing else, but he didn't need to, and she realized what he meant. Because Philip was the only other person to whom Julia had seemed real.

"How can you grieve someone you never met?" she whispered.

Philip touched her cheek. "You did meet her, Winnie. She was inside of you, and she was as real as anyone. Just as you gave her a name, I pictured our future together as if it were truly going to happen. She was as much a person to me as she was to you, but I don't think you've ever allowed yourself to believe that."

She didn't know what to say then because there were tears in his eyes, and she could feel his pain as if it were her own. This time she held him as he cried, and together they lay like that through the night, grieving a baby they'd never had, a future they'd never seen.

They must have dozed because the next she realized she was chilled again, and the sound of rain had ceased. The dovecote had a single window, and it was lit with the watery gray light of early dawn. She nudged Philip beside her, and together they dressed, her gown and chemise blessedly dry now.

They didn't speak. It was as though they had said the last of what needed to be said between them in the small hours of the night inside the dovecote. When they emerged, it was to find the tide receded, but the salt marsh boggy with mud. Philip held her arm as they traversed it, cutting a path back the way they had come. The wind had settled, and sounds were sharp in the near silence. The call of a bird, the rasp of reeds, and the soft cadence of the sea far away.

They had made it back to the main road when the sound of footsteps met them. They both looked in the direction of the turn toward town, and Winnie supposed neither of them were surprised to see her father and Robert making their way down the road, walking sticks in hand as if prepared for a muddy salt marsh trek. She raised a hand, and her father broke into a run, abandoning his walking stick as he made a dash for her.

Her heart squeezed with guilt that she had caused him such worry. The apology was already on her lips when her father reached her, but instead of apologizing, she just let him hug her, the events of the last day coalescing around her until she couldn't tell one memory from another. She wanted to apologize for her foolish behavior, for running off like that, but then she remembered Philip's words about grieving.

They had somehow gotten mixed up in her mind with Mathilda's words about pushing people away, and she wondered if she hadn't been carrying on these past five years or simply hiding from herself. Did she push others away because she really wanted to push herself away? And what was she running away from? Grieving? But grieving was her right.

Instead she said, "I'm so sorry, Father. We got caught in

the storm, but we found shelter in an old dovecote. I didn't mean to worry you so."

Distantly she heard Robert greeting Philip who was assuring the man that all was well, and that they had weathered the storm just fine.

Her father let go of her long enough to study her face to see if she was lying, likely. She smiled, and even though her eyes were gritty with unfit sleep and tears, she felt she meant it. Her chances of marrying Chichester and saving Ingrid were at absolute zero now, but she felt lighter than she had in years.

"Your mother was ready to write the prime minister," her father informed her. "It seems Robert and I are not adequate rescuers for her." Here her father stepped back and elbowed the other man who laughed good-naturedly, and Winnie's heart ached at the sight of it.

Had she ruined this? Her father and Robert got on so well. Would there be nothing more now? Would the Clarkes withdraw what little support they had offered for the union?

Winnie didn't know, but she was suddenly tired of blaming herself.

It was in that break of greetings that Winnie's stomach decided to growl, and her father peered at her in concern.

"I think perhaps it's time to return," Winnie said, taking her father's arm and steering him back in the direction of the village and the hotel. "How are the guests? Have they all recovered?"

Her father shook his head. "Recovered and demanding Chichester give them back the money they paid for the pleasure of it."

Winnie looked swiftly at her father, her stomach tightening. "No," she breathed. "But his entire enterprise here could be ruined."

"Yes, it probably will be." Her father gave her a pointed look, and she knew the thing he wasn't saying.

She patted his arm. "Don't worry, Father. I don't think Chichester will be of concern to us any longer."

Her father's eyebrows went up. "Is that so?"

She didn't like the way he looked quickly behind him at Philip. Was there hope in her father's gaze? Expectancy?

She kept her eyes focused on the road. "I'm afraid after last night I shan't be receiving a proposal from him."

Father scoffed. "Then it should only be further reflection of the man's character. Instead of thinking the worst of you, he should be thinking of your safety."

"He should be out here himself." Winnie was surprised by Robert's words. The man was always jovial and considerate to others, and it was startling to hear such a harsh statement from him, and she regretted anew how her actions would affect all of their futures.

They were outside the hotel when Philip finally spoke. She had hoped nothing more would be said about their night in the dovecote, but she knew Philip would not let the matter go.

"Lord Bibury," Philip said, stopping them under the portico in front of the main entrance. "I want you to know I plan to ask for Winnie's hand. I don't wish for you to worry about the matter."

Her father looked between Philip and her, his brow creased.

She rushed to fill the space. "Father, I assure you there is no reason for Lord Greylock to offer for me. It was all a terrible accident, and if anything, he should be commended for all he did to keep me safe during the storm." Her father raised a single eyebrow, and she knew later she would pay for such an airy statement, but she rushed on. "I shan't accept an offer from Lord Greylock. He's done nothing to make such an action required."

She didn't wait for a reply and, dropping her father's arm, pushed into the hotel. The lobby was packed, even more so than the day they had arrived, and she suddenly realized the state she must be in. Her gown was likely ruined. She'd finger combed her hair into the resemblance of a plait, but she had no hat, and her slippers were little more than a suggestion of footwear. She must have been quite the sight to the guests.

Chichester towered over the assembled crowd, his voice raised to be heard above it as he spoke nonsense words she thought were meant to be soothing to his agitated guests. It did nothing to calm them, however, and she saw a barrage of assorted gentlemen in matching jackets who were likely staff going around to individual guests with ledgers and coin purses.

She waited, knowing Chichester would see her eventually. She had drawn a great deal of attention from those guests closest to her, and she noted the whispers now circulating. But it wasn't until Philip stepped through the door behind her that Chichester finally found her, and even from this distance, she watched his eyes grow cold right before he turned his back on her.

That was how it was to be then. Not that she had thought it would be any different.

Before Philip could approach her, she slipped through the crowd, her eyes searching. She knew Philip. She knew he would press his suit. He would think it was the right thing to do. He would think he was saving her. She didn't need saving. She never had. And if she did ever require saving, she would choose who would do the saving.

She stepped around the main staircase and caught sight of Ingrid. She was standing with the Clarkes, and they were speaking in hushed voices, too far away to be heard, but

Ingrid saw her. Winnie was hard to miss unfortunately, and something strange passed over her sister's face then. Winnie wasn't sure what it was. She had expected anger. After all, Winnie had ruined the last chance for Ingrid to marry the man she loved, but it wasn't that. It was something fiercer. Winnie couldn't think about it then. There was someone she needed to find.

Finally she spotted her. Genevieve's coppery red hair shone through the crowd like a beacon, and Winnie went to it. Her friend was speaking to a pair of women Winnie didn't recognize, but Winnie tapped her on the shoulder anyway, gripped by a sudden urgency to see this through.

Genevieve turned, a curious frown on her lips at the intrusion, but then her face opened into a bright smile. She went to speak, but Winnie spoke first, saying the only thing that needed to be said.

"I'm sorry," she said right before Genevieve pulled her into a bone-crushing hug.

CHAPTER 13

Three days later Philip stormed through the front door of Hodge House tracking road dust across the glistening marble floors of the foyer.

"Sheldon!" His call for the butler rang through the quiet confines of the foyer, and he stopped his progress abruptly, his greatcoat swishing around him.

He stared down at it, memories pouring at him like an insistent waterfall, and he ripped the thing from his body, tossing it to the floor.

"Sheldon!" he called again, and again, but was met with silence.

Where the bloody hell was everyone?

It had taken longer than he had anticipated to settle Grandmother Regina and Aunt Verity back at the house on Grosvenor Square, and it was nearly evening now. He desperately needed a bath and a fresh set of clothes. His valet had gone around the back with the carriage and was probably now unloading his trunk, but where was the damn butler to fetch him a bath?

Philip would go to Lord Bibury that very night and plead

his case. Winnie must see reason. He had compromised her. They must wed. Even now she could be carrying his child.

The thought had him stopping again as he made his way deeper into the house.

Could she be carrying his child?

He held out a hand, pressed his palm flat to the wall beside him. Oh God, what had he done? What if she lost the baby again? What if…

He straightened and lengthened his stride. He had to get to her. He had to marry her. If she…if it happened again…

No, he couldn't think like that. She would be all right until he married her, and then he could take care of her properly. She wouldn't be alone again to carry the weight of such tragedy by herself.

He was nearly to the rear stairs that would lead down to the butler's office when noise at the front of the house stopped him. He swung about, prepared to give Sheldon a lashing for not being at his post, when his sister stepped into the corridor from the main staircase.

"Philip, what on earth are you bellowing about?"

The light from the windows that flanked the front door gave her a soft halo, and she suddenly seemed much younger than she actually was. His heart twisted at the sight of it, remembering that she was to be married now. Already marrying when he had neglected her for so long.

Time was passing around them all like sands in a windstorm wearing edges that seemed impenetrable.

She took a step closer to him, her hands loose at her sides, her head tilted. "I thought you were with Grandmother."

He retraced his steps to the front of the house as he said, "We've just returned."

Her expression was inquisitive. "How was it?"

Philip thought of all the guests still ill from the brackish water that remained at the hotel and thought it unlikely to matter for long as the news would be dwarfed by the demise of Chichester's venture entirely. "It's irrelevant, I'm afraid. Where is Sheldon?"

"It's Tuesday." His sister's voice was wondering. "Philip, what's happened? You're not yourself."

He shook his head. It couldn't be Tuesday. Could it? But that would mean the servants had the afternoon off. Damn and blast. He pushed past Caroline as he headed for the stairs. This only meant he would need to make do without the bath.

He took the stairs two at a time, Caroline's voice ringing out behind him.

"Wait. You must tell me what's happened. What is wrong?"

He should have slowed. It would have been the polite thing to do, but he wasn't feeling particularly polite. Urgency gripped him. He had to make Winnie see reason. He had to get Lord Bibury to accept his suit.

Again.

The thought had him stumbling on the upper floor landing as it suddenly occurred to him that he'd done this before. Five years ago he had made a journey across Surrey to press his suit to Winnie's father, and here he was again, attempting the same thing.

The man had done the same then as he'd done the previous morning in Sutton Cross. He'd let his daughter make her own decision in regard to whom she would marry. Blasted man. He should have made the right choice for his daughter, and even now, Philip could be applying for a special license.

His momentary stumble meant Caroline caught up to him, and now she grabbed his arm, holding him back.

"Philip, you must stop, or I'll get Hawk."

Hearing his best friend's name gave him a jolt as he

remembered the man would soon be his brother-in-law. Philip peered down at his sister, noting the line between her brows and the worry in her eyes.

"I asked Winnie to marry me, and she refused."

Caroline released her death grip on his arm, her mouth working without sound emerging. He took the opportunity to attempt escape, but she latched on to him again.

"What are you talking about? You were supposed to be taking Grandmother Regina to try the waters." She shook her head, her eyes suddenly huge. "How does this involve Winnie?"

Philip knew if he didn't stop and explain everything to his sister she would continue to pester him, so he paused, right there in the corridor, and told her everything.

He told her about the maze at Lady Satterwhite's garden party, he told her about the invitation to Sutton Cross and why he had taken Grandmother Regina there instead, and finally he told her about being stranded in the dovecote with Winnie. He didn't tell her what they had been doing while stranded there, but he figured if she were marrying Hawk she might already know what might have happened there. The thought made him sick to his stomach, and if Hawk weren't his best friend and if Philip couldn't have imagined a better husband for his little sister, he would think seriously about calling the man out.

Caroline stood perfectly still next to him, her eyes unmoving as she absorbed what he said.

"So there you have it," he finished, holding his arms out as if he had made everything perfectly clear.

Which apparently he hadn't because then Caroline said, "So why are you in such a hurry now?"

He crossed his arms over his chest. "Because I must go to Lord Bibury and make him see reason. Winnie cannot refuse me. She *needs* a husband." He emphasized his words, hoping Caroline would understand their meaning.

But he couldn't stop the image of Winnie that night in the dovecote from floating through his mind. The way she had looked, crushed as if she were finally broken into so many pieces even he couldn't put her back together. But maybe if he married her, he'd at least have a chance.

Caroline pursed her lips and shook her head. "Oh Philip," she breathed, her forehead wrinkling in what might have been pity.

He dropped his arms and took a step back, his nerves prickling at his sister's countenance. "What is that look for?"

Caroline shook her head. "You're only making it worse the more you speak."

"Caroline."

She drew a measured breath as if preparing herself. "Have you ever asked yourself if you love Winnie?"

Remembering that night in the plunge pool, the word was like a dagger directly to his chest. "Why is that important? Winnie needs a husband and—"

Caroline held up both hands. "Stop saying needs. Please. You speak of her like she's cattle, and you're the benevolent farmer seeing to her sustenance."

It was his turn to frown. "That is not at all how I see it. I am helping Winnie. There is nothing wrong with—"

"Philip, you're not helping. You're controlling."

The words stopped his own as if his sister had cut out his tongue.

"I am not controlling."

"You haven't thought about what I said, have you?"

He blinked, and he knew it was the incorrect response. Caroline threw up her hands and paced away, only to come railing back at him. "I told you before you left that you needed to consider whether or not Winnie wished for your help. If you haven't noticed, Winnaretta Lowe is a strong, capable woman in charge of her own destiny, and she doesn't need you meddling in it." Here she poked him in the chest like the annoying little sister she was.

"I am not meddling. Winnie doesn't understand the dangerous position she's put herself in. She needs a husband, and I will marry her."

Caroline grabbed hold of his arms. "Philip, she doesn't need a husband. She can take care of herself."

"I am helping, Caroline."

"Stop saying that. You're not helping. You're making it so much worse. Can't you see that?"

The muscles at the back of his neck tightened as the pain in his chest grew heavy, and breathing became difficult. "I don't have time for this conversation. I must see Lord Bibury—"

"Philip, no. I won't let you ruin this. If you truly love Winnie and wish to marry her, you cannot press her on this. She must make her own decision, and you must trust her to make the best decision for herself."

Philip was already shaking his head and tugged at his arms to break Caroline's hold. "No, I can't. She doesn't know what she's doing. She's too young."

Caroline's face folded in confusion, but he was too busy trying to yank his arms free without tossing his sister down the stairs for the look to register.

"Stop. You must—"

"Caroline, let go. I need to—"

"Philip, please. I can't see you hurt again. You—"

The pain and turmoil inside of him erupted then, words spilling from his mouth before he could stop them, his hands finding Caroline's arms as if he needed to hold on.

"I must, Caroline, because I need to protect you."

Silence.

They stared at each other, and Philip felt his heart racing as though he'd just finished a race he hadn't known he'd been running. Caroline's grip on his arms loosened as her jaw slackened.

"Oh Philip," she whispered, but he couldn't think of anything else to say.

The sudden space in his chest was too large—the words he'd never spoken finally opening a cavity inside of him. He sat down, collapsed really, on the top step of the staircase, and let his head fall against the polished wood paneling, the tension of the past few weeks colliding with a pain he'd buried deep for so many years.

He heard the rustle of skirts and knew Caroline sat beside him even before she touched his arm.

"I'm sorry, Philip," she said, her voice soft now. "It wasn't your job to protect me."

"Don't apologize, Caroline. I shouldn't have needed to protect you." He opened his eyes then and allowed himself to look at her.

But he wasn't seeing his sister who was about to be wed. He saw his sister as a young girl, her hair still in braids when their mother first discovered their father's infidelity, and their home became a minefield of screaming matches between their parents, Philip and Caroline drifting between them, afraid to make too much noise in case it might set one or both of them off. He may have been at school for most of it, but he still knew. He'd just tried his best to ignore it, and by ignoring it, Caroline had gotten hurt.

He shifted and put his arm around his sister, drawing her against his side. "I'm sorry, Caroline, if I have tried to control your life. It's not what I intended. I hope you realize that. It's only that I regret not being here with you when things got really bad."

She gave a soft laugh. "I must apologize to you, brother. I'm not really one who will allow herself to be controlled."

Philip laughed then. "God save poor Hawk."

They were quiet again for several seconds before Philip asked, "Are you sure about Winnie? I can't help but feel she's making the wrong decision."

Caroline eased out from under his arm to look at him. "You told me once that you loved her. Is it still true?"

Philip knew of the moment Caroline spoke of. Had it been mere weeks ago? He had found her sulking in the garden folly and exchanged a secret for a secret. He had admitted how much he had been in love with Winnie when she'd broken off their engagement five years ago, but now, having seen Winnie again, he knew his feelings then were nothing more than infatuation, a boy's dream about his future and the possibilities with a woman as extraordinary as Winnaretta Lowe.

Now, though, he knew that infatuation was only the beginning. His feelings for her ran deeper, steadier than the heady throes of early love, truer than the fickle nature of lust.

He met his sister's gaze and spoke the only word that mattered. "Yes."

Caroline wore her heartache on her face as she said, "Then you need to let her make her own choice."

* * *

THE FIRST MORNING upon their return to London Winnie woke up wondering how long she could hide in her rooms.

She had spent her last day in Sutton Cross holed up in her room with Genevieve. There had been tears amidst confessions and lots of tea and biscuits, and in the end, Winnie had taken a breath deeper than any she had in five years.

She breathed now as she lay in bed, willing time to stretch

a little longer even as she wondered when real life would intrude once more. After all, there was still the matter of Ingrid and Robert that must be solved.

The answer to how long until life intruded was three seconds because that was how long she lay there before an unholy pounding sounded at her door before it was thrust open, and her mother came stampeding in.

"She's gone!" Ada Lowe was not one to bellow, but bellow she did just then.

Winnie sat bolt upright, her heart racing from the sudden movement and her mother's cry.

"Who's gone?"

They had arrived back in London the previous night, and it had been unusually cool, so Winnie had pulled an extra quilt onto the bed. Now she regretted having to untangle herself to gain her feet as her mother scurried around her room.

Scurried?

Lud, something was terribly wrong. Her mother still hadn't answered her by the time Winnie stood, her bare feet sinking into the carpet, and she went to her mother who was throwing back the curtains as if she could find whoever was missing behind the panels of velvet. After two futile attempts at getting her mother's attention, Winnie simply latched on to her mother's hands, preventing the woman from opening another blasted curtain.

"Mother, what is the matter?"

"Oh, it's terrible, Winnie." Her mother's face was blotched with angry red welts, and her eyes looked as though someone had rubbed sand into them.

Winnie blinked, her heart rate doubling. She'd never seen her mother so upset and instinctively she looked around the room for Mathilda. The woman stood just inside the bedchamber, her hand still on the dressing room door where she'd presumably been getting Winnie's things ready for the day. The maid's eyes were wide in concern, but her lips were thinned in determination. Winnie's heart rate slowed considerably just seeing the woman.

"What is terrible, Mother?" Winnie tried again to get her mother to elaborate. "What could possibly be so wrong?"

Mother pulled her hands away only to grab Winnie's shoulders in a bone-crushing grip. "Robert and Ingrid have eloped."

It was a full ten seconds before Winnie's brain properly interpreted what her mother had said.

"Eloped?" She laughed. She couldn't help it. The idea was simply too ludicrous. "Ingrid wouldn't do…"

But she didn't finish the sentence. Somewhere in the deep recesses of her mind came an image of her sister that last day at the hotel when Winnie had stumbled in, her dress ruined with salty mud, Robert's parents speaking too far away for Winnie to hear their words but their faces so stern she didn't need to hear what they said. And Ingrid, standing amongst them, her eyes on Winnie, her face set. No, not set. Resolved.

"Oh no," Winnie breathed and searched behind her for the bed, her legs unsteady, only to have Mother snatch her back.

"Now is not the time for lounging, Winnaretta," her mother nearly spit with authority. "We must do something."

Winnie blinked as if the movement could force her thoughts into some order. "Mother, how do you know she's eloped? Maybe she's just walking in the park or…"

Her mother moved so quickly Winnie was nearly knocked directly in the chin as her mother pulled a folded piece of paper from between her breasts. Winnie reared back, surprised her mother used her bosom for such a purpose and also slightly disconcerted to be handed a piece of paper that had so recently been there.

"She left a note." Mother's tone was calmer now, and Winnie took the paper so as not to upset the woman again.

She unfolded it and quickly scanned Ingrid's looping handwriting. The note was simple. They'd eloped.

"To Gretna Green of all places," Winnie muttered.

Mother threw up her hands and spun away from her. "I know! The girl couldn't even have been original."

Winnie looked up from the note. "What would have been original in terms of eloping?"

"Scandinavia."

They both looked to Mathilda as the woman gave an affirmative nod.

"Yes, that would have been original," Mother muttered.

"But far too chilly for Ingrid." Winnie refolded the note. "You know she doesn't like to be cold."

Mathilda seemed to consider this and gave a shrug as if the cold were of no concern.

Winnie turned to her mother. "Well, what is to be done about this? I'm sure Father has an idea."

Mother waved a hand as if she couldn't even believe Winnie would suggest this. "If he does, he hasn't been able to utter it."

Winnie frowned. "Why on Earth not?" Her father was not the emotional sort, and having a daughter elope was not the first potentially scandalous thing one of his daughters had ever done, so it shouldn't have made him speechless.

Her mother pulled at the lapels of her dressing gown, and Winnie realized the woman must not have been up for very long before she'd learned of her daughter's elopement.

"Because he's too busy trying to calm down the Clarkes."

Winnie went cold. "The Clarkes?"

Mother gestured to the floor. "They're in the drawing room spouting off nonsense about how Ingrid has ruined their virtuous son." Here Mother held up her hands as though she were exclaiming to the heavens. She dropped her hands and turned to Winnie. "That's how we knew they had eloped. Lord and Lady Snowshill arrived nearly a half hour ago demanding we do something about our daughter." Mother laughed a pitiless laugh. "Do something. About Ingrid." She threw up her hands again. "Like we haven't tried!"

This was Winnie's fault.

The thought rolled over and over in her mind like the waters in a whirlpool constantly churning, the same thing repeating. If Winnie hadn't—

No, she couldn't tarnish that day in the dovecote. She would cherish that moment forever.

If Winnie hadn't failed to secure Chichester's proposal, this wouldn't have happened. Ingrid and Robert wouldn't have had to elope. All would be well. Winnie had failed the people she loved. Again. She must fix it.

She snatched up her dressing gown and flew to the door, forgetting her slippers entirely. She was halfway down the stairs before she got the belt secured around her and then it was only a matter of steps into the drawing room where her father was apparently being admonished by the Clarkes.

The scene that greeted her was so alien Winnie froze on the threshold of the drawing room.

Her father sat in a chair in the corner by the Leonardo da Vinci bust, holding his head up with a fisted hand as he leaned on the arm of the chair. His eyelids were thick and droopy as though he'd been suddenly awakened from a very deep sleep. He hadn't shaved, his cheeks spectacled with white and gray hairs, his overly long white hair sticking up in places, and his dressing gown was tied asymmetrically so one side of his collar jutted into his ear.

Winnie collected the image of her father sitting there looking utterly defeated and put it with all the rest she had collected over the past few weeks—the things she thought she would never see and some she never wished to see again.

Now she stepped forward neatly when Lady Snowshill drew a breath in the middle of an apparently exhausting tirade, if her father's stature were anything to go by.

"Lady Snowshill." Winnie kept her voice calm, hoping it would have a desired effect on the woman. "I understand something is amiss."

Lady Snowshill had clearly taken the time to dress before coming here to barrage the Lowe family with her accusations. Winnie knew they were accusations because of the tightness of the woman's face. If the viscountess's lips grew any thinner, they would disappear entirely.

"Your sister has corrupted my only son!" She yelled this.

She yelled this at such a decibel as to have Winnie stepping back and nearly colliding with her mother and Mathilda who had just managed to catch up to her. Winnie shook her head to stop the ringing in her ears and stepped fully into the room, folding her hands neatly in front of her while pretending her feet were not bare and she was not wearing little more than a nightrail as she conducted this conversation with the irate viscountess.

"Lady Snowshill, I assure you my sister has not—"

"Do not dispute the facts. Your sister has manipulated my son into—into—"

Winnie worried for a moment the woman was choking as she made a terrible phlegmy sound deep in her throat.

Lord Snowshill stepped in and took his wife's arm, patting her back gently. "My son is the victim of your sister's scheming, and I will not allow the Snowshill title to suffer from her immoral ways."

Winnie glanced at her father, but it looked as though he were pretending to have fallen asleep, or perhaps he really had fallen asleep. It was hard to tell.

"Lord and Lady Snowshill, I think it would be best if we remain calm at this time. We do not have many facts with which to work. We have only Ingrid's briefest note of their intentions and nothing of their motivations. It would be wise to refrain from such accusations until more is known."

Lord Snowshill puffed up like an irate walrus. "Are you suggesting my son is the one at fault here?"

"I'm suggesting your son is guilty of nothing more than falling in love, and he should not be condemned for it." She smiled to soften her words. "I am sure we can all understand such an affliction."

She meant the words lightly, but Lord Snowshill suddenly appeared as though he were having an apoplectic fit.

"No son of mine shall be disgraced by falling in love! How dare you suggest it?" He waved an arthritic finger at her, spittle raining from the fan of his bristly mustache.

Winnie leaned back so as not to be sprayed and waited for the man to settle, but instead of continuing, he turned to his wife. "I told you we should have been more careful when Robert expressed an interest in that girl. We knew what stock she came from, and we acted recklessly in not destroying the association at the outset."

The muscles at the back of Winnie's neck tightened. "You knew what she came from?"

Out of the corner of her eye she saw her father rouse and knew then he'd been feigning sleep, but the viscount's words had his attention now.

Winnie took another step forward. "What precisely do you mean by that?" Her pulse raced, beating a tattoo in her neck.

Here it was. The pronouncement of her failings. Finally it was happening. Someone was declaring the worst part of her as truth. Her weakness of character called out for all to see. The reason her sister was now not planning her wedding to the man she loved but instead harrying across England like a criminal bent on escape.

Winnie pressed her hands to her stomach, wishing Julia were there, wishing someone was there who—

No, she couldn't think of that now. Couldn't think of the comfort she had found with Philip, the support and peace. She was alone now and would never have such peace again. She had to remain strong.

But then Lord Snowshill turned and said, "Your father belongs in Bedlam. Everyone knows it."

Winnie opened her mouth, her rebuttal already on her lips, but then—no…wait…what…

She shook her head, her mind a scrambled mess. "I beg your pardon?"

Her father rose slowly from the chair and came to stand beside her. She could feel the tension radiate from him and wondered if she would be forced to stop him from physical action. But then she became aware of Mathilda stepping clear of the threshold, one fist kneading the palm of the opposite hand, and Winnie said clearly, "I do hope you did not intentionally mean to insult my father."

Snowshill took a threatening step toward her, and Winnie could all but hear Mathilda's jaw clench.

"The evidence of your father's insanity is clear for anyone to see in every preposterous facet found in this house." Snowshill flung his hands wide to encompass the drawing room. "And your sister's actions are further evidence of the deficient strand that runs through your family." He swiped at the air as if to emphasize his point.

Winnie blinked three times, letting Snowshill's words sink in. "You think my family is…defective?"

Snowshill wiped at his mustache as if more spittle had become adhered there. "It's quite obvious, I should think. You're the most normal of the entire lot. If Robert had chosen you for his childish infatuation, I might have gone along with it."

Most. Normal.

The past several weeks condensed into the flash of a second then, speeding before Winnie's eyes as if it were happening all over again. The maze with Philip, Julia, Philip wishing to choose their baby's first pony and thinking it would be a boy, the grief that had overcome her at seeing her best friend again, her pregnant best friend, the pain and the terror and the hurt telescoping until she thought she could never breathe again and then…finally…peace.

She waited for it to slip away from her, fleeting as peace had always been in the past five years. But it didn't go away. It stayed, warm and solid and permanent.

At some point in Snowshill's speech, Mathilda had come to stand on her other side, and she leaned forward in the Clarkes' direction as she said, "Do you wish for me to take care of them, my lady?"

Snowshill's eyes widened, and for the first time, Winnie saw a spark of fear in them. She realized Mathilda had spoken in Norwegian, and Snowshill likely didn't know what she had said.

Winnie smiled, and her shoulders straightened without effort, suddenly freer than they had been for five years. "No, Mathilda. I'll handle this."

Mathilda's head turned sharply, her fist stalling in the opposite hand. Winnie felt her assessing gaze, but she could only continue to smile as she approached the Clarkes.

"Lord Snowshill. Lady Snowshill." She addressed each in turn. "Excuse me."

She was halfway to the door before Lord Snowshill spluttered, "What are you doing?"

She paused and looked over her shoulder at him. He stood in the same shocked tableau next to his wife, his eyes squinting in anger. She turned fully as she said, "My family doesn't waste time with unsupported accusations, Lord Snowshill. We are a family that seeks action and factfinding over pandering and gossip. So if you'll excuse me, I'm going to do something about this while you stand here and waste time thinking up more unfounded and unflattering adjectives to use against your own son." She bit off the last word, and before the viscount could find his tongue again, she left the room.

CHAPTER 14

He had gone a measly forty-eight hours and had already come to a conclusion about his sister's advice.

She could stick it in her hat.

He lay on the sofa in his study contemplating the plaster medallions of the ceiling. He had decided one cluster looked suspiciously like an elephant while the other looked more like a rhinoceros. Despair had set in hours ago, and the fact that he should be contemplating the plaster medallions of the ceiling concerned him hardly at all.

Hawk had arrived sometime the day before, likely summoned by his soon-to-be-wife. He wondered suddenly if he should be concerned with how easily he thought of Caroline as Hawk's betrothed. It just seemed so right that he hardly considered it. It was quite simply perfect.

He'd spent the majority of the past few hours reliving the moment on the stairs with Caroline and wondering what else might be lurking beneath the surface. His outburst had surprised him, yes, but there was something more to it than that. It had him rethinking his actions for the entire past five years of his life.

How much had his parents' estranged marriage affected him without him realizing? How had he inadvertently allowed this to affect his behavior toward others?

Hawk had tried to assure him the effects were minimal, but Philip wasn't so sure. Caroline had been so desperate to get through to him that day, and it wasn't as though she hadn't tried before then.

He felt like a failure, lying there on the sofa. He had failed Caroline, and now he had failed Winnie.

Was he doomed to never get out of his own way?

Hawk had again claimed this to be nothing more than Philip's own self-degradation, assuring him that he hadn't let down anyone. If anything, he had responded with courage at every opportunity.

Philip had just begun to outline a walrus when the sound of the front door opening trickled through the open door of his study. He wouldn't have given it further thought, assuming that Audrey had come to see Caroline about a matter concerning his sister's forthcoming wedding, but then different noises followed, ones that sounded entirely like a heated discussion taking place in the foyer.

He picked up his head, his gaze riveted on the door as if he could hear better by looking in the general direction.

"My lady, please. I shall see if he is at home before—" But Sheldon's words were drowned out by the stampeding of feet.

A very light and delicate stampeding of feet.

Using the back of the sofa, he levered himself to a near sitting position at the same moment Winnie flew through the door.

"She's gone," she said without greeting. "Ingrid and Robert have eloped."

He swung his feet to the floor and stood in a single motion. "They've eloped?" He wasn't sure how Winnie's hands ended up in his or how he had even crossed the floor to her, but the need to touch her was as pressing as the need to breathe just then. "How do you know?"

"She left a note." Winnie pulled her hands free of his then, and he let her as she reached for her reticule, rummaging inside of it before brandishing a folded piece of paper.

He took it from her and unfolded it, reading through the short note quickly.

"Gretna Green. How terribly original. When did they leave?" His mind was already several steps ahead before he realized what he was doing. He tried to rein in his thoughts, his sister's words shuddering back to him, but this was Winnie. He'd never been strong when it came to Winnaretta Lowe.

She needed his help, but he gritted his teeth, waiting for her answer.

"This morning, we think," she said. "I don't think she would know to go anywhere else." Winnie licked her lips, her eyes roaming his face as if she were trying to decide what to say next. It unsettled him. What could she possibly need to say to him that had her so visibly nervous?

"Philip, there's something else I must tell you."

Oh God. If he gritted his teeth anymore they'd simply shear right off.

"You know you can tell me anything, Winnie." It felt absurd to say it. Hadn't they already been through so much together?

She licked her lips again and grew even more worried.

"I was never in love with Chichester." She released a breath, and her shoulders dropped.

He waited for surely there was more, but when she didn't speak again, he said, "Is that it?"

Her eyes searched his face, her forehead wrinkling in confusion. "Yes, that is it." She shook her head. "What do you mean? Were you expecting something else?"

He shrugged. "I already knew you didn't love Chichester. I've told you as much."

She took a step back, her eyebrows going up. "I thought you were trying to make an argument. How did you know? I said—"

He couldn't stop a laugh then. "Winnie, my love, you can never keep the truth from me. I know you better than I think you know yourself." He realized too late what he'd said.

My love.

He watched her eyes widen, her lips parting softly, but before she could take another step back, he gripped her hands, holding her in place.

"Winnie, I love you."

She shook her head. "How can you still say that?"

"Because I still feel it. I have loved you probably since that first day we met. Do you remember?"

She didn't say anything. She only watched him, her eyes wondering, her lips still parted.

"You were standing in the field of wildflowers, and the sun was shining on you like you needed its warmth most." He shook his head, unable to stop a smile as the memory formed in his mind. "You weren't wearing a bonnet, do you remember? And your hair was—" He had raised his gaze to take in her beautiful hair and realized she wasn't wearing a bonnet now. He hadn't noticed in the confusion of her entrance, but now he paused and took her in. She wore no bonnet nor gloves, and her gown looked as though it had been trampled by a carriage. "Did you dress in a hurry?"

She frowned. "It seemed prudent not to waste time."

Fear and not a little bit of embarrassment seized him then. He swallowed and released her hands. She was in crisis, and he was spouting nonsense about how he loved her. Caroline was right. He really couldn't see clearly when it came to the people he loved.

"Right," he finally said. "That was probably wise." He looked around him if only to clear his head. "I assume your father has left for Gretna Green then?"

Her frown grew fiercer. "I'm afraid my father has been delayed. The Clarkes are at the house now. There was a bit of a situation."

"Situation?" His mouth began to lift on one side, and he forced himself to remain serious. "Was Mathilda involved?"

Winnie raised her chin. "Actually I handled it myself."

It was his turn to take a step back. "You did?"

Her eyes narrowed defensively. "Why do you sound surprised?"

He shook his head, wondering at the woman who stood before him. When he had first met her five years ago, she had been reserved, young, and almost biddable. It hadn't been surprising considering the situation he had found her in. He couldn't imagine the grief she must have been feeling then, the enormity of the world and what her condition meant for a lady at the time. But somehow he wasn't at all surprised to see she had grown into the woman who stood before him now. Strong, capable, unbending.

It was everything he loved about her.

"I was just wondering why it took you so long to realize the strength you have inside of you."

Her expression melted then into one of uncertainty. "You think me strong?"

"I think you're a lot of things, Winnie. Strong is only one of them."

She licked her lips again, and he wanted nothing more than to pull her into his arms, but she seemed so unsure then, and he worried she'd reject physical comfort.

"What other things?" She said the words in a rush, and something shifted inside of him, seeing her like that, so vulnerable and raw.

The uneasiness he had been feeling since he'd heard of her impending engagement that day on the viewing platform came roaring back then. "You're brave," he said quickly, hoping to finally learn what it was that really drove her to such a dangerous action as to marry a deplorable man like Chichester. "You're courageous and caring and unselfish. I've never seen anyone give up so much for someone else like you do every day for Ingrid."

Winnie looked away and back. "Ingrid does require a lot, I'm afraid. I don't think she can help it."

"And you're never one to cast blame at someone else's feet, no matter how deserving they are."

Her eyelids drooped then as if she couldn't look at him any longer, and he reached out, lifting her chin with one finger so she was forced to meet his gaze. "You're extraordinary, Winnaretta Lowe. You're extraordinary in the all the little ways that people overlook, but it's those little things that truly matter, and you see that. You've always seen that, and that's why I love you so terribly much."

Her eyes wandered over his face, and he wondered what she was looking for, but then she said, "You don't think me…" She closed her eyes briefly as her voice drifted away, but when she reopened them, he saw a determination there. "You don't think me weak of character?"

Somehow he knew the question to be an important one. The fierceness of her eyes, the directness of the question, the way she held her chin just slightly higher, so his finger was no longer holding her head up, it all shouted at him to be careful. There was something here, something important to her. Perhaps the very reason she had nearly doomed herself to a life of misery.

"I don't, Winnie," he said simply. "I don't think you weak of character. If anything, I think your character is one which should be aspired to. You lead with unselfish intention, and that is a rare quality in a person." He felt the words stab at him and his own weakness, and it was his turn to look down now, studying his feet as he collected himself. When he finally returned his gaze to her face, it was to find her watching him curiously. "Some of us do not have that ability, I'm afraid. We think we're trying to help, but really we are only trying to force an outcome we desire."

Her eyes widened, and he knew she understood what he was saying, but it wasn't enough.

"I'm sorry, Winnie," he said. "I'm sorry I tried to force my suit on you. I thought it was the best for you, and part of me has always regretted how things ended between us. But now I understand the only one who can know what is best for you is you. Just know that I will always be here should you need someone."

He stepped back then, severing any remaining connection between them.

She watched him carefully for a moment before she spoke again. "That's actually why I'm here, Philip." Her voice was so soft he almost missed her words. But the next part, he heard quite clearly. "I need you to save my sister."

"Save your sister?"

Winnie stepped toward him now, her eyes earnest. "You'll be faster on horseback than my father could be. If anyone has a chance of catching them before they make a terrible mistake, it would be you. Please, Philip. I need your help."

He thought of Caroline's words, of the defeat that had overcome him when he realized what he had done, but now Winnie stood before him. Asking for his help, her words and intention clear.

"I'll leave at once," he said.

CHAPTER 15

She wasn't sure what they would find when they finally reached Gretna Green nearly a week later, but it was certainly not the tableau into which they walked.

It had taken them an interminable time to reach their destination. Her mother had insisted upon packing everything that may be of use even if it seemed they would most definitely not require it. Father's alpenstock for example. What did she plan to do with that? Impale Robert? Hardly. It was more likely she would use it upon her own daughter.

They'd broken a carriage wheel before they'd even reached Leeds. They limped the carriage into the nearest village, and then it was a matter of finding a blacksmith to fix it. It had taken him most of the day, and they were forced to wait for the repair, losing another day of travel.

But after assessing the situation into which they walked, it seemed impalement was not in order.

The Pheasant and Hound was a small pub, but it seemed the central street of Gretna Green was littered with them. It was clean as far as Winnie could tell with the odd ring stain on a table top here and there, but the floor was swept clean, and the air was thick with yeast. A fire roared in a fireplace to one side, and a group of old men had drawn chairs about it in a half circle as if to take in its warmth while they chatted. Except they'd turned the chairs about now and faced the spectacle occurring in the middle of the pub.

Robert faced off with Lord and Lady Snowshill who looked as though they'd just arrived, road dust around the hems of Lady Snowshill's skirts and creases in the backside of Lord Snowshill's jacket. They had not wished to share a carriage with the Lowes, and Winnie was grateful for it. She had feared what her mother might do with the alpenstock before they reached Scotland.

Winnie's father stepped up to them immediately. "I should like to know what is going on here."

Winnie had never heard her father speak in such a ponderous tone, and she wondered if he'd once used it on his students at the university before he'd inherited the title. She held her mother's arm, afraid the woman would surge into the pub and demand retribution. It had taken a great deal of negotiation to get her to leave the alpenstock in the carriage after all.

As they approached the group, Winnie caught her sister poking her head out from behind Robert. Winnie closed her eyes briefly. It was just like her sister to hide behind someone when pressure descended. Nevertheless, Winnie only hoped they had arrived in time.

"Bibury," Snowshill said, tugging at the lapels of his coat.

Winnie stilled, her other hand going to her mother's arm. Snowshill appeared nervous, shuffling his feet against the wooden planks of the pub floor. "It seems we have arrived in time. Nothing has been done that cannot be undone."

Winnie released her breath, allowing her shoulders to relax. She relinquished her mother's arm but only after she gave the woman a knowing look. Her mother attempted to appear innocent, but it didn't matter. Now that she knew the wedding had been stopped, there were other more pressing matters.

She swept her gaze over the pub in front of her, but except for the gentlemen gathered round the fire, it was largely empty. A woman with two small children sat to one side, their heads bent over a meal of pies and potatoes as if oblivious to what was happening around them. A pair of gentlemen occupied stools at the bar, and another woman filtered through the tables, wiping them off and gathering empty tankards.

They had arrived sometime between noon and dinner, and Winnie was grateful the entire populace wasn't in attendance to witness her family's private matters in the middle of the pub.

But where was Philip?

"It seems I owe you an apology, Bibury," Snowshill said.

Winnie turned her attention back to the group, the muscles at the back of her neck suddenly tightening. What was this? Snowshill was apologizing to her father?

While the man owed several people apologies, she'd never expected him to actually deliver one. But he did then, holding on to his lapels as if for courage.

"I'm told a Lord Greylock stopped the wedding. Robert said he's a friend of yours." Snowshill bent his head, appearing properly ashamed. Winnie worried she might be gaping. "I also wish to thank you for acting so quickly." He shifted his gaze then to Winnie, and she straightened her shoulders under the scrutiny. "It appears you've raised one competent young woman, and it's led me to believe I may have been too critical in my previous judgment of your family."

At a complete loss for words Winnie looked between Snowshill and her father.

Where was Philip?

Snowshill stepped forward and offered her father his hand. "I should like to discuss a marriage contract with you upon our return to London."

Her father hadn't even accepted the man's hand when Ingrid leapt out from behind Robert, releasing a squeal of utter delight.

Father crossed his arms over his chest and glared at his youngest daughter. "Lord Snowshill, I am glad to see you've had a change of mind, but I'm afraid my daughter shall not be accepting a marriage proposal this season. It appears she has some more growing up to do."

Ingrid's eyes expanded to the size of saucers while Robert almost lurched forward in disbelief.

"My lord," he said. "I...I...assure you it was—"

Father raised a hand before Robert could take the blame. "Clarke, you are a good man. Probably too good for Ingrid, and I commend you for wishing to shield her from what's about to happen, but I cannot in good conscience allow you to marry a woman who does not understand the consequences of her actions. Ada." Her father didn't turn to face his wife as he said her name but kept his gaze on Ingrid who seemed to be frozen. "It seems our daughter requires further finishing."

"Father, no!" Ingrid's voice was wet with petulant tears. "You cannot do this."

"I can, and I shall." He turned back to Snowshill and took the hand the man still held out. "Lord Snowshill, I shall be happy to entertain your offer in the spring. You have my word on it."

Snowshill appeared just as astonished as poor Ingrid. "Yes, right. Thank you, Bibury."

Father released the man's hand. "Now then, how about some ale? Bloody long journey from London, wasn't it?"

Snowshill mumbled something as he nodded and began to follow Winnie's father to the bar.

"Wait, please." Winnie managed to rouse herself from the unexpected scene before her. Snowshill and her father turned toward her, and she said, "Where is Lord Greylock?"

Snowshill pointed to the door. "He left when we arrived. He said as long as we were here he was heading back to London."

"No." She didn't know why she said it, and everyone looked at her as though she were mad, but it was as though her brain had figured out something she hadn't quite grasped yet.

But it didn't matter. She picked up her skirts and ran back out to the main street, letting the door of the pub slam shut behind her in her haste. She asked a passing couple for the location of the stables, and they pointed farther down the street. It didn't take her long to find the place, and without waiting for a groom to see her standing at its entrance, she pushed her way inside.

It was darker there amongst the stalls, the ground soft with discarded hay and the air thick with the odor of manure. She scanned the space before her, but the stalls were too tall. She couldn't see if anyone was inside of them saddling a horse.

There was nothing to be done. She must check every one of them. Luckily he was in the fourth stall she tried. Not so luckily his horse jerked forward as soon as she opened the stall door as though he might bolt, and without thinking, she stepped inside, snapping the stall door shut behind her.

Philip pinned her with a glare as he caught the horse's bridle and attempted to calm it after her sudden intrusion.

"I'm sorry," she said, pointing to the horse. "About startling your horse." She stopped to catch her breath, her hands braced along the walls of the stall as she tried to compose herself after her run. She took in the horse then and realized why Philip had glared at her. "That is an enormous horse." She could only imagine the destruction the beast might have caused.

"Thank you," Philip said. "I picked him up in Carlisle. I'm thinking of keeping him."

"Picked him up?"

Philip rubbed the animal's neck, making soothing noises. "Yes, I swapped horses. That's how I was able to get here so quickly."

Winnie stared, imagining the cost Philip had incurred with such a practice. It would also require him to swap horses on the return journey unless he really did intend to keep this beast beside them. But then, what would that cost him?

She shook her head, scattering the unnecessary thoughts. Tentatively she eased away from the stall door. The horse bowed its head, sniffing her hair inquisitively.

Philip smiled. "I think he might like you."

She held up a hand, careful to keep her fingers flat as she let him sniff her. He nuzzled her hand before returning to her head, butting her playfully at the temple. She laughed and pulled her head out of his reach.

"I think you might be correct." She grew serious then as she took in his traveling clothes. "Philip, I must thank you. I can't imagine what you went through to get here in time."

He shook his head, but there was something sad about his eyes that worried her. "It was nothing, Lady Winnaretta. I am always here to help you." He moved then as if to ready his horse to leave, and suddenly she understood what she had only just realized standing in the pub.

She stepped forward, stopping inches from Philip, and said, "Marry me." Philip stilled, his gaze focused on hers, but he didn't speak. She kept talking, afraid to let the silence grow. "Marry me. Right now. Here."

He raised an eyebrow. "In a horse stall?"

She laughed, unable to stop herself. "No, I mean in Gretna Green. Marry me. Today. Please." She stopped speaking then because she had said all she needed to say.

Philip let go of the horse and turned fully to her. She noticed then the darkness under his eyes, the gaunt look about his cheeks. How hard had he ridden to get here in time? What had she put him through? God, it had been so much. So much before this last hell-bent ride to Gretna Green. So much. And she would spend the rest of her life making it up to him.

"If I recall correctly, you refused my marriage proposal. More than once." His eyes were dark with emotion, and she couldn't look away.

"I was wrong." She licked her lips, her mouth suddenly dry. "I was wrong, Philip. I thought I had to marry Chichester. Not just for my sister but because I deserved it." His eyes changed then, guarded and defensive, and she rushed on before he could interject. "I thought it was my fault. I thought I was weak of character because I fell in love with you five years ago." She laughed, the idea suddenly so absurd and ridiculous and magical. "I fell in love with you when I thought I couldn't feel anything ever again, and I thought that made me the worst kind of person, but it doesn't. It didn't." She swallowed, feeling tears, but she knew she had cried enough in the last week. "I wasn't weak of character, Philip. You were right. My only shortcoming was in not allowing myself to be human. A human with feelings and desires that don't always fit with who we think we should be. But that doesn't make me weak. It just makes me, me."

"I like you," Philip whispered then, a smile tugging at his lips as he watched her.

God, she could get lost under that gaze. Every day for the rest of their lives, she hoped he looked at her like that. With such wonder. With such love.

"I like you too," she whispered in return. "I like you so much I love you."

His face changed, hardening into something else, and for a moment, she felt panic.

"Winnie, I owe you an apology too. I'm sorry I tried to stop your engagement to Chichester. I had no right to interfere like that no matter how much I care for you. How much I love you. I promise I will try to be better in future to trust you to know what's right for you, but I need you to tell me when I'm overstepping." His grin then was sheepish, and it tugged at her heart. "I'm not very good at knowing when I am."

"In future?" she asked, almost too scared to hope. "Does that mean you accept my marriage proposal?"

"Yes," he said. "But only because I'm so bloody tired of proposing to you."

She stood on tiptoe then and kissed the smug look right off his face.

CHAPTER 16

*M**any years later...*

SHE WATCHED as the negotiations intensified. The stakes were high, she realized, and she knew the parties involved were equally as tenacious in achieving their goals.

"I want that one."

Winnie did her best to hide her smirk as her six-year-old daughter repeated the same sentence she had already repeated three times.

Philip crouched beside their daughter, his hands resting on both of his knees as he looked through the slats in the paddock fence. "But you already selected a pony, Gigi."

Genevieve was undaunted. "That pony was for Freddy."

Philip glanced back at Winnie, eyebrows raised as if to ask if she were listening to this tale their daughter was weaving. Winnie only smiled in response, bouncing the aforementioned Freddy on her hip as he grew bored of the pony negotiations and wished to simply stomp about in the mud puddles in the drive.

Freddy had just turned three and had no interest in ponies beyond watching them trot about in their pens, but Genevieve persisted.

"Freddy likes brown ponies. That's why I chose that other one for him," she said, referring to the pony already being brought round for them to take home. Genevieve pointed at the pony now in the paddock. "I like black ponies. I shall have this one."

Philip glanced back at Winnie again, and this time she was unable to stop the laugh that came to her lips. Philip's gaze intensified, and he tilted his head as if he couldn't believe she would laugh at him.

He went back to the negotiations. "But we're only getting one pony today, Gigi," he said, and Winnie's heart tightened at his use of the pet name he'd chosen for their daughter.

When Winnie was pregnant with Genevieve, he'd come up with the shortened name one night as they lay in bed, his head resting on a pillow by her stomach as he talked to the baby. This time it was he who was convinced it was a girl, and as they had decided on the name Genevieve if it were a girl, he'd started referring to the baby as Gigi.

She'd laughed off the pet name as she was sure it was a boy. It was quite a shock when the baby emerged a girl, and suddenly her daughter was known as Gigi by everyone except her. She had resisted at first, but the look on Philip's face at his triumph was enough to have her warming to the name.

She could admit now how terrified she'd been carrying Genevieve. At first she couldn't quite believe she was pregnant again. Somehow she had thought she was broken after losing Julia. But it seemed her body understood what to do. It didn't stop Winnie from spending whole days in bed,

fearing that if she remained upright the baby would acciden-
tally slip out.

Philip never made her rise and go about her day. Sometimes he even joined her, and they would spend the whole
day in bed, arguing over baby names and godparents.

Robert and Ingrid were Genevieve's godparents, of
course. The first Genevieve had graciously acquiesced when
told the baby would bear her name.

Robert and Ingrid had eventually married, of course.
Even now, Winnie was surprised by her sister's tenacity at
staying the course even against their father's reprimands. It
seemed Ingrid was finally good at something.

Genevieve's face grew serious. "But Father, you have two
children. Please tell me you wouldn't buy a pony for only one
of them."

Philip's expression blanked in obvious surprise at his
daughter's acuity, and in clear retreat, he stood, shaking his
head. "You're right, Gigi. How silly of me to think of only
getting one pony today."

He made his way over to the paddock to instruct the
groom they would be taking both ponies that day. Gigi ran
ahead to greet the ponies as they were brought round to
their cart, her squeals of laughter cutting through the crisp
fall air.

"Stay with Mathilda," Winnie called after her daughter.

Mathilda retrieved Freddy before chasing after
Genevieve, and Winnie caught the soft sounds of Norwegian
the maid murmured to little Freddy as she set him down to
finally splash through the puddles he so coveted. The entire
thing caused the air to stop in Winnie's throat, and she
pressed a hand there as if to quell the rush of happiness.

Mathilda had been only too happy to return to the
nursery when Genevieve was born, and Winnie couldn't
imagine anything more perfect than to have her children

cared for by the same woman who had so fiercely protected her. Still protected her, really.

Philip made his way to her, scratching his forehead with a look of deep resignation on his face.

She pulled his arm against her. "Cheer up, love," she said. "It could have been far worse."

Philip dropped his hand. "How worse?"

Winnie couldn't stop the devilish smile from coming to her lips. "She could have known about the babe I'm carrying, and then you'd be buying three ponies today." She patted his arm and walked away before the shocked expression could dissolve from his face.

"Winnie." His voice was stern and imploring all at once, but she continued to follow in the footsteps of her children and Mathilda, her smile growing ever wider as she heard her husband scampering along behind them, trying to catch up. "Winnie, what babe?"

Finally she had mercy on him and turned, her hands going to her stomach. "Let's hope it's another boy. You're not very good at negotiating with girls."

This time she let him catch her, and when he kissed her, she knew without a doubt just how lucky she was. No. Just how lucky *they* were.

ABOUT THE AUTHOR

Jessie decided to be a writer because there were too many lives she wanted to live to just pick one.

Taking her history degree dangerously, Jessie tells the stories of courageous heroines, the men who dared to love them, and the world that tried to defeat them.

Jessie lives in New Hampshire where if she is not at her desk writing, she's probably letting the dog out. Again.

For more, visit her website at jessieclever.com.